I0771848

MERMAIDS AND LAZY ACTIVISTS

A Lake Michigan Tale

MAUD LAVIN

Published by
From Beyond Press | Chicago, IL
frombeyondpress.com
mike@frombeyondpress
Instagram: @from.beyond.press
Bluesky: @frombeyondpress.bsky.social

ISBN: 979-8-9875743-6-2
Library of Congress Control Number: 2025932986

Contents

Episode 1
The Mermaid and the Crib

I have always wanted to meet a mermaid. Maybe they're legends grown from manatee sightings and longing, maybe women in diaphanous, emerald-green evening gowns who prefer a night swim to one more minute at a cocktail party, their kicked-off silver shoes left shining on the shore. And maybe unicorns are narwhals, only that. I don't think so, because I have a friend who's seen a unicorn, walking side by side with death, as he tells it. Maybe mermaids are women who prefer the buoyancy and acceptance of water, the wavelets that lick them all over, to the tedious gun-toting people on dry land.

I never really knew till I made a trip out to the Crib off 57th St. beach sponsored by the Water Reclamation Board. I begged off the tour once we got there and sat outside on the walkway, staring out at the endless lake while the rest went inside to see the giant water pumps. Evelyn came swimming over. First, I thought, my God, this woman has come all the way from Promontory Point! Must be over two miles of Lake swimming, what is she, Olympian?! Like a lot of the big deal swimmers on the Lake, she had quite the getup, a shimmering body suit all the way down to her flippers. And her face was glowing and bronzed.

"Hi, I'm Evelyn," she said.

"Your skin looks great," I said to her in that girl-to-girl Midwestern compliment way.

"Oh, thanks, I exfoliate with tiny mussel shells. Drink a lot of water, too. Hmm, your skin looks nice also, for a landlubber, ha ha."

Oh, I thought, she's a Midwesterner as well, knows how to return a compliment. "Thanks, I drink a lot of water and tea."

"Do you have a Melitta filter?" she asked.

"No, probably should get one."

"I found mine on the shore at night, that's where I get most of my stuff."

"You live on the lakeshore?"

She laughed, "I live in the Lake. I'm a freshwater mermaid."

Well, I almost fell over. Having revealed that much, she flipped away with a "nice-meeting-you, see-you-around!"

"See you, take care!" I waved.

Episode 2
What's with Evelyn

I'm back at the beach, 57th Street beach, natch. It's 88 beautiful degrees out, Labor Day weekend, the swimming is *chef's kiss*. This is the last weekend for the lifeguards, and they are on the case, rowing parallel to the beach, making sure we all stay near the shore. I'm even with the lifeguard rowboat, far enough out that I can breaststroke back and forth, back and forth, dreaming and dodging the waves. I've heard recently that I'll likely need knee surgery, but out here my knees, both of them, work just fine, thank you very much, and I feel strong. General anesthesia, my ass, I intend to refuse it, holding out for local. No one is fucking with my head. Except for me, and my man Bruce, and the Lake, and chocolate edibles. Only those people and things I love are allowed in there. I love the Lake. I try to let go of the imaginary conversation I'm going to have at the surgery consult with my doctor, and I reach up and out, up and out, frog kicking my legs, feeling my round stomach stretch long and muscled. Then, I'm not even thinking at all, just swimming.

The lifeguard in the rowboat yells my way, "Too far out! Get back."

Seriously? I'm right even with her. I stop, treading water, looking around. Oh, there's a long-haired woman out further than me, swimming in tandem with me, except she's, wow, doing the butterfly, and let me tell you, she's good. That dolphin kick. And strong arms out to the Y-shape and then down into the water lifting her chest up. Powerful! She's making it look easy and I know it's not. Wait, I recognize the shiny green outfit.

"Evelyn!" I call.

She doesn't want to stop, but she turns her head toward me at a high chest-lift moment and gives me a big smile and a wink. Then a dive and she's gone.

That Evelyn.

Episode 3
Evelyn Confers

Fall has ripped in. The trees on Promontory Point have changed to reds and oranges, with remnants of greens and nips of bare branches showing. And through the gaps and under the branches, always the Lake. To the right, to the left, and through the front-center views, the Lake. Bruce has gone off on the Lake trail for a run, and I'm ambling around the Point. Come up to the rocks fronting it, the sugar-cube pile where brave souls jump off to swim in the summer. Climb down to a nice, steady flat one for perching. I hope Evelyn will come by. I want to show her the outfit I wore for her—long black sweatshirt over silver mini-scale tights.

No dice, though. So, I make some notes on my phone for the eco-poem I want to write about salt dumping in the Lake. How to write with hope and humor and not just scolding, I don't know.

"Synthetic!" I hear, yelled at me from the water.

There's Evelyn! I didn't see her at first. She's wearing what seems to be a seaweed helmet and her scales are now black with red highlights. A new outfit.

"Hey, Evelyn! Good to see you!"

"You're not impressing me with those synthetic scales, you know," she responds.

"I'm not trying to impress you, hon, just flashing some beauty your way," I say.

She tells me I'd make a cute mermaid.

"Ah, thanks," I reply.

Evelyn wants to know what I'm doing.

"OK, maybe you can help me. I want to write a poem or maybe a short story against salt dumping in or near the Lake, but I want it to have some fun elements in it too, in addition to the dire message of how the Lake is being tainted by the salt runoff. Why don't we write it together?"

"Really," she says, "why?"

"Well, that's one thing I do with friends, I like to write collaboratively, and I think we could be friends. Also, you know, you live in the Lake. Maybe you can add some personal touches. Like, why you don't like salt in the freshwater."

She sighs. "I thought we could talk girl talk about dating and so forth. Well, yeah, I'd love to."

"First, this, though, OK?"

"OK," Evelyn says, "too much salt can kill off freshwater fish, so that's bad. Also, it's deadly for some kinds of underwater plants. See this helmet? This is vintage, made of seaweed, one of the things that keeps me warm in the Lake in the winter. (Of course, the quagga mussels have already eaten most of the seaweed.) Salt ruins the water for drinking—for mer-people and humans. What's more is that salt in the Lake makes my beautiful skin all puckery. Which leads us directly to the topic of dating."

I laugh. "Alrighty then. So, how do you 'date' in the Lake?"

She replies in her contrarian way, "hon, we don't know each other well enough for those details." Wink. She likes the winks.

Evelyn continues, "I'll tell you that I'm into landlubber men these days, they're so exotic. And some of them, honestly, not that bright. But eager. It doesn't even occur to them that I'm a mermaid, just that I'm willing."

"I'm not following—how do you even meet them?"

"Well, I can switch to legs for periods of time, so if there's a guy hanging out on the beach at night, getting stoned or whatever, and he looks cute, I arrange an appearance." She giggles. "In the summer, I wear only a woven beach-grass bathing suit. Other seasons, well, I still show some skin. We chat for a little while, and if the guy has condoms on him, chances are he gets lucky."

"Well, aren't you a bold thing! So, you like sex but you're not looking for a relationship?"

"Yeah, I like to play."

"You're worried that if your face gets puckery, landlubber men might not want to play with you?"

"Yeah," Evelyn admits.

"Well, I say, my face is a little puckery from getting older and a man—my husband Bruce—still plays with me. Maybe you don't have to worry."

Evelyn laughs. "This is what I'm talking about. Real girl talk. OK, I hear you. I still don't want extra salt in the Lake though."

"I hear you too, sis."

Evelyn blows me a kiss and she's off.

Episode 4
Evelyn and the Gourmet Food Tour

Still fall, still leaves on the trees on Promontory Point, but fewer. I'm now dressed in a purple sweater over a purple midi dress of a different shade and reddish-purple cotton tights with sneakers. What does that have to do with the story, you might ask. Nothing. A great outfit is worth noting. It contrasts nicely with the green, baked pea pods from Trader Joe's I'm scarfing while reading, sitting on one rock, my back to another.

"Nice 'fit," says Evelyn, swimming up.

Well, see? It does have to do with the story after all—an icebreaker.

"Ah, we're snacking," says Evelyn.

She dives down, seaweed helmet and all. Comes back up with a medium-size fish in her mouth. "What's that?" I ask. She holds up one hand as if to say wait a minute. The fish is wiggling but she bites its head off, chews and gulps the treat, and then more slowly savors the rest.

Ugh, it was still alive. I make a face.

"Oh, please," she says. "Gotta enjoy these, we can only have one per week. It's a whitefish."

"Why is that, the one a week thing? Trying not to deplete the whitefish population?"

"Nope, it's because they contain pollutants."

"Oh."

"It's the same restriction for humans," she explains, "even though we mermaids have larger and more effective livers cleaning our systems. But we want to be careful, too, you know."

Evelyn looks entirely comfortable, not even cold, in the water. "Listen, I've got to tell you, I may not be around for a few weeks."

"Where are you going?"

"Well"—pause, lifted eyebrow—"I'm going on a gourmet eating trip with a mer-group."

"Really, huh, I don't really see you traveling with a group, you seem so independent."

"Yeah, I am, but it's safer."

"I don't travel alone anymore either because I hate to drive so I go with Bruce and he drives. Also, you know, I like Bruce."

"Who's Bruce?"

My God, Evelyn is so self-absorbed. "I already told you—he's my husband. He's around the Point right now, too, doing his running."

"OK, is he cute?"

"Yeah, he's delicious."

"Ha," says Evelyn.

"You can't have him, he's mine."

Evelyn frowns. I'm a little worried because I sense how rebellious Evelyn is. Changing the subject, I say, "so tell me about this gourmet trip."

Evelyn brightens. "Oh, it's going to be great. We're swimming up to the top of Lake Michigan, then into Lake Huron, which you know is the same lake. This is a long distance, even for us, so we're going to really let it rip getting up there, and it's going to feel great."

"Amazing," I say.

"We then take a left to get to Huron's North Channel, replenish on some coho salmon, rainbow trout, whatever else we feel like. Rest up a bit before doing the rapids on St. Marys River. This is where we need the group safety." She halts dramatically.

I'm more than happy to play her straight woman. "Why?"

"I'll tell you why. The river goes for 75 miles and there's a 23-foot drop. There are locks, too—we switch to legs and walk around the locks. Anyway, it's a tricky waterway, sometimes shallow, sometimes with sinkholes, tons of rocks, vicious rapids between the Canadian city of Sault Ste. Marie and the American one, and other places in the river—and idiotic fishermen everywhere. We try to go at night when they're not out, but then it's harder for us to see. We take turns being scouts, sending warning noises back to the group."

"The fishing hooks can hurt you?"

"Yeah, those are no fun, but more of a nuisance than anything. We've got very sharp incisors that can bite off a line, and we can help each other get the hooks out without too much damage. The worst thing is that if the fishermen see us, they might try to collect us or alert other humans. Or distract us as we navigate the rapids. We're strong but the river and the rocks are still dangerous. We need to focus and we need our strength. We can't eat the entire time we're in the river."

"Wait, you're not worried I'll report you?"

"Nope, you're harmless."

"Oh, OK, well, you're right, at least as far as you're concerned. I know some humans who might not agree," I add to save face.

Evelyn wants to continue her story. "I'll tell you why we can't eat," she says with authority. "St. Marys is polluted as fuck, pesticides, polyaromatic hydrocarbons (PAHs), and other carcinogens. Even with our excellent livers, we can't eat the fish around there. And there are so many fish! They all have to channel through there if they're traveling. I remember when we could find safe spaces among the rocks and chow down to our hearts' content."

"When was that?"

"Oh, like 100 years ago, thereabouts."

"What? You look about 35."

"Nah, I'm older than you. We live a long time, if we're lucky, about 200 years."

She looks at me. "You won't live too long."

"I know," I say, "I eat too much cheese. And I should get more aerobic exercise."

"What? No, you look fine, I mean just because you're human."

OK, Evelyn shrugs off the mortality talk and continues her story. "Finally, we'll get up to Lake Superior, Whitefish Bay. We'll get far enough away from the river, the settlements, whatever, and then, mmmm, eat and eat."

"It's cleaner up there?"

"Well, polluted up there, too, but less so. For humans you're not supposed to eat the fish often, but we mer-people can still go pretty wild in Superior. It's too cold for me to enjoy living there all the time, but for vacations . . . !" She makes a chef's kiss.

"I love Lake Superior, too," I offer. "I've only been swimming in it once, in a small inlet off the coast near the Apostle Islands. So clear, to the bottom, I loved every minute."

"Very, very wonderful," says Evelyn, nodding and listening for once.

We're both quiet for a minute or two, staring north over the water.

Episode 5
Evelyn Writes a Poem

The knee surgery came and went. I lost the battle with the doctor about general anesthesia, but, in any case, it wasn't the scary kind with a tube down the throat, instead a mask full of laughing gas or whatever. And I came through fine. Some time cooped up at home after, and finally here it was late November and I could go out. As long as I took it easy.

Bruce and I swaddle up and drive down to 57th St. beach. He helps me set up a folding chair near the water's edge. Bruce wants to stay to see if he could meet Evelyn too, but I say no way. That mer-girl is all id, and Bruce is too much of a snack. Fine, he's off for another run. (Reader, get you a man who enjoys running.)

No sooner has he disappeared north on the lakeshore path, than boom there she is. Sporting black scales with red highlights down her legs and two bare human-looking feet, a black puffer jacket that seems dry, a new-to-me helmet of shiny blue fish scales with some sort of padding underneath. Long, streaming brown hair. Radiant face. Wow, she's tall up close.

"Evelyn! So good to see you," I say. "The cold agrees with you."

She plops down in the sand. I hand her the beach towel I'd brought. "Here, in case you want to wrap this around your feet." She shrugs, takes the towel anyway.

"How can your jacket be dry?" I ask.

"How can you ask so many questions?" she answers.

"That was one question, Evelyn."

"OK, so, I brought you a present from my trip," she says.

"You're kidding!"

She hands me a long, wide, flat roll of what I think is underwater plant leaves with a long line of words on it. "You like poems, right?" she says, trying to act cool. "Well, I wrote you one. It's also a recipe, one of Malcolm's. But I made it more poetic."

"Oh, I love this!"

"You haven't read it yet."

I hold the scroll up close. In beautiful cursive, the writing says:

Lake Superior Fish Stew, for a Human Friend

Brook trout, dusky, pottery-glaze-blue skin with white oblongs—
they call it vermiculated.
Who cares, bite the head off, or use a knife,
if you're a weak human.
The skin is the best part, but if you're a
weak human, cut it off since the fat underneath
stores pollutants. (So does the fish flesh, but the skin more so.)
Shake the flesh off the bones. Don't eat it yet, you piggy little human!
Bite or cut it into bits.
Next, take two coho salmon, look at those
mean snouts, those dayglo red and green colorings
on the skins. If you're a wussy human,
cut off the skin. Do NOT eat the meat yet.
Chop it all, except for the head, up.
Mix the salmon bits with the trout bits.
If you really must, cook it.
Eat it all in one sitting. Your tummy
will feel great. Shut up.
The end.

"Evelyn, I don't know what to say. Not keen on the name calling parts, hon—but otherwise it's a wonderful gift. Thank you!"

"Oh, you're welcome. Malcolm helped me."

"Who's Malcolm?"

Evelyn blushes.

"You're blushing!"

"No, it's the cold."

"Well, who is he?" I ask.

"He's a merman and he was the leader on the gourmet group eating trip. He loves to eat, and so do I."

I notice when she talks about Malcolm, little red sparks jump off the black scales on her torso. "Evelyn! You have a boyfriend!"

She gives me a quelling look, but I see she's still sparking.

"Anyway, how are you, little human?"

"Oh, I had a knee operation. I'm doing OK."

"Next time, ask the doctor to turn your legs into a mer-tail."

"Well, you know, I spend most of my time on land."

"Yeah, too bad. You look good though. Your face looks happy."

"Yeah, I am—things are going pretty well."

"Look, I gotta get back in the water and meet up with Malcolm. Try the recipe, let me know next time how you like it." She hands me back the towel. It's completely dry, too. Takes delicate steps, then a giant leap and a whoosh, she's waterborne. A quick handwave and she dives down.

I hold the towel close. There's no sand on it. I worry I might be imagining it all. But that's not possible. I know Evelyn exists. And her poem in old-school cursive is still in my hand.

Episode 6
Back on the Beach, and the Bad River Band of Lake Superior Chippewa

It's a climate-change fluke of a day. Deep fall, but the air is in the upper 70s. The water is colder. I'm wading in the water on the sand shelf at 57th St. beach. The beach is closed, technically.

"Hey, what are you doing?" It's Evelyn. For one confusing moment I think she's in cahoots with the lifeguards, and then I remember they're gone till next summer.

"What am I doing? Whatever I feel like!"

"OK, I thought human flesh started to freeze at these water temperatures."

"Nah, I'm all right, just grumpy about you always sneaking up on me. Anyway, Evelyn, I have a question for you."

"Good, I have one for you, too."

"Me, first: I've been wondering, why do you and Malcolm have these British names?"

"Well, they go back," she says with a sigh. "Before the Europeans came, it was us in the Lake, and many different tribes of Native Americans on the land or traveling via the Lake and the rivers. Chippewa, Menominee, Sauk, Fox, Potawatomi, so many. We couldn't quite figure out who was in alliance and who was in competition, so we kept to ourselves. For the most part," she added with a small smile. "Ahem, well, I have to admit that back then, one of the Chippewa (Ojibwe) clans was the Nibiinaabe or merman clan—their totem had a human torso and head and a fish tail body. So, we may have intermingled a bit. In any case, under the surface, our names were sounds for us alone, sounds that carried well underwater. Then, in 1634, a very snotty French trader showed up, and then more French people, each one with that snobby moué and complaints at occasional fireside outdoor meetups that our food wasn't well sauced (we didn't make any sauce). We don't like snobs, so we tried to ignore the French.

"Then in the 1700s," Evelyn continues, "lots of British people came. They were mean to the Native Americans, which we didn't like, but also mean to the French, which we did. We figured that they were going to run things for a while—having built Fort Mackinac and so on. I'm skipping a lot here, suffice it to say, we thought they might leave us alone if they thought we were also British. So, the names, and, for a while when we were around them, we used fake accents, too. The names stuck."

"But their faces were likely pale, and yours are bronze-ish—didn't they think you were Native Americans?"

"Ah, well, we told them it was from living outdoors.

"Meanwhile"—Evelyn was getting impatient—"fast forward a couple of centuries. I got interested in the Bad River Band of the Lake Superior Chippewas. I mean, the name alone, right? And they had excellent recipes, lots of land. I got to know one guy, I think it was in the mid-20th century, who was really into collecting agates, and I even helped him find some." She looked away. "Family name Moder."

"You're kidding!" I say. "I have a friend named Tim Moder, a poet, and he's from the Bad River Band. Lives in northern Wisconsin. He's been down to read his poetry at the READINGS series I run at Printers Row Wine."

"Hmmm," says Evelyn, "he might be my friend's grandson? Well," she pivots, "this all fits in with my question—how do I get my poems out there so I can be a famous poet?"

"Um," I caution, "hardly any poets are famous, more just hang out in bars, maybe teach some, or work some other jobs. But the READINGS are fun. And there's wine." I tell her more about the READINGS series and the wine bar.

"So, now that I write poems, I could read at the wine bar, too!"

"Evelyn, it's, like, you've written one poem?"

"I'm working on some more! Really, I just want to read my poems, maybe kick back with a glass of wine." There's that wink again. "You know you want to invite me." She presses her case more.

I give in. "That sounds great. Bruce and I could come pick you up and drive you to the bar, bring you back here after. You'd get to hear my writing, too—I don't just run the series, I sometimes read as well. Um, maybe this is the time I should admit I've been writing some about you."

Evelyn laughs, "I knew you would! What I think is funny is that your human listeners will think you made me up, but actually I'm real! Ha, humans. OK, I know, like this: you read some stories about me the same day I come up to read my poems, alright? I'll wear some human clothes. Trust me, they'll never figure it out."

"Bruce will know, and what if Tim Moder is there and you tell some old stories about his grandfather, woven into your poems—should we tell him?"

"I dunno—let me meet him first. But in general, it's all a secret, OK, missy?"

"OK! Sure, what could go wrong?"

Episode 7
Evelyn Reads at the Wine Bar

Waiting near the entrance to Promontory Point, Evelyn is a sight to behold. She's dyed her hair black, with the front sections left long, braided around what looks to be beach grass, the rest up in a messy bun in back. She's wearing a black beret, a long off-the-shoulder black sweater, a full, shiny black skirt, and no shoes. She's got a lot of black make-up around her eyes, and bright red lipstick on her mouth. She stands over 6 feet tall.

"Evelyn, hi! You look gorgeous, right out of the East Village, 1982! Quite the poetess. Very punk."

As for me, I'm wearing the silver scale tights and a black sweatshirt tunic on top, with sneaks. Bruce has on Dockers, a black Henley, and sneaks.

"Oh, this is the first time for you two meeting," I say. "Bruce, Evelyn, Evelyn, Bruce. Evelyn, hands off my man, I'm not kidding."

"Please," she says, "I live for my art." She beams at Bruce.

Evelyn's face is glowing as usual and she looks more Amazonian than urban artist, but that's all to the good.

"I like your outfit too," she says to me, smiling, "it has just a hint of mermaid about it—you look very fetching." I smile back.

I'm a little worried that Printers Row Wine won't be able to let her in barefoot since they serve food there. "Evelyn, I think Bruce can lend you some sneakers so you won't stick out."

"Really? Poets wear sneakers these days?"

"'Fraid so."

"Okey doke."

Inside the bar, there's a huge turnout. That's the way it is sometimes, standing room only. I'm glad to see so many people. And very glad Bruce and I are wearing masks. Evelyn pulls on her mask too, black and shiny, perfectly matching her skirt. I think maybe she looks a little like Diane Seuss, if Diane Seuss were a mermaid, broad shouldered and tall, and dyed her hair stone cold black, which, you know, she probably does.

I'm in the glow. Busy circulating, saying hi to people, I lose track of Evelyn, catch only a glimpse of her drinking a glass of wine "under her mask" and talking with poet Tim Moder by the bar. Uh oh, I've never been around an imbibing Evelyn, I realize. But am too busy to worry much.

The event starts! I've put Tim second and Evelyn third, right before intermission. Tim is reading some of his nature poetry, and transports all of us listening right to the woods near the Lake Superior shore. Then he reads one about finding agates. Evelyn is practically levitating!

It's Evelyn's turn. I introduce her as an emerging poet from the shores of Lake Michigan, dripping with talent. She steps up to the mic, takes down her messy bun, and shakes out her hair. I see there are more grass-braided strands in the mix. She takes the mic out of its stand. Takes her mask off to read.

"Hello, little humans!" she declares. "Lemme tell you something." She shakes out her waves some more and starts her first poem.

> *"Fuck Monsanto!"* she booms, *"Fuck polychlorinated biphenyls!*
> *Fuck PCBs!*
>
> *Outlawed by humans in 1979, still carried into the Lake*
> *when it rains. When it rains, little humans! Do better!*
> *Let's hear it for Mayor Brandon Johnson and the City of Chicago,*
> *now suing the fuck out of Monsanto and Bayer.*
> *Fuck PCBs. Shut up!!!"*

The crowd is on its feet. Evelyn has brought punk back to the South Loop! We applaud.

I look over at Tanya, the wine bar owner, and Lee, the wine director, and they're cheering her on.

"For my second poem," Evelyn says in a quieter voice, "I'm sharing with you some of the pleasure of a Lake swim."

"I call this,

Liquid Prayer to a Great Lake

Buoy my joints, float my limbs,
blur my hair, soothe my face,
hold me near, sing to me.
Living water embrace me, take the stiffness
from my spine, from my knees, the
weight from my shoulders, lift
my breasts, stay, stay, stay.
Move me along, scare me some,
feel my arms stroke your surface,
love me, push me, still me. Don't let me go.
I don't want to leave the Lake, don't want the burning land.
I stay afloat, I stay moving.
Keep me smooth, keep me safe."

I think I see a few sparks fly off Evelyn's clothes. I shut my eyes and think of swimming in the Lake.

And finally, she says, "Maud likes it when I share some poem recipes, so here's one for all of you."

That's nice, I think to myself.

"Salmon Patties

Catch three kinds of Lake Michigan-planted salmon
King Salmon, Coho Salmon, Atlantic Salmon.
Bite the heads off, spit them back into the Lake.

(Her voice starts to rise.)

Peel the skins off with your teeth, rip
out the bones. Take the flesh in your two hands
or flippers. Or, hell, use a mixing bowl.
Massage the glistening flesh pieces
together. Eat them raw, humans, eat them raw!
Fuck the phosphorous runoff, the agricultural chemicals,
Fuck all that plastic shit you dump in the Lake, eat
the salmon raw!"

"Eat it raw! Eat it raw! Eat it raw!" she's yelling.
She points the mic at the audience, waving their voices up.
The wine-fed audience yells it back,
"Eat it raw! Eat it raw! Eat it raw!
EAT IT RAW! EAT IT RAW! EAT IT RAW!!!"

Episode 8
Early Winter Evelyn

I'm wearing, like, a million layers. Bra, undershirt, thin sweater, blanket sweater, down coat with lavender polka dots, two hats, two pairs of socks, gloves. There aren't many other humans on Promontory Point these December days, just some diehards taking their constitutionals. The leaves have almost entirely left. But Evelyn is not fazed. Cheeks pinked, hair still dyed black, black puffer jacket still mysteriously dry, two seaweed helmets, one on top of the other. We're sitting on the rocks a ways down to shelter from the wind. Evelyn has brought a hot thermos of tea.

"This is delicious," I say. "I'm not even going to ask how you got this, it tastes that good."

"Oh, I don't mind telling you. I belong to a spa that we made out of some abandoned basement rooms below that Crib."

"Wow."

"Yeah, it's all fitted out. We can heat up drinks. Also, there are computers and e-readers in dry rooms we can use if we sign up in advance."

"You're kidding."

"Nope," Evelyn says proudly. "The e-reading room has pillows and everything. Some of us didn't like it though because at first there was a rule you had to switch to legs in the dry room, and legs aren't that comfortable for relaxing. But now they've put in a little stream and pond at one end. If the room's not too crowded you can stretch out with your mer-tail in the water and the rest of you plus the e-reader lounging on dry pillows."

"Amazing."

"So, speaking of computers. I Googled your personal name, Maud, and it's British, too."

"Yeah, it is. British with no e, French with the e at the end," I reply.

"So, what's with you and the Brits?"

"Well, it's interesting. I think when I was born in the 1950s my parents wanted to assimilate and so they chose aspirational names for my brothers and me. Aspirational to WASP norms."

"So, you tried to seem British like we did!"

"Kind of. I'm Jewish, and there's a certain amount of negative prejudice here toward Jews. We're a minority—only about 2 percent of the US population. Some Jews want to blend in more, they have surgery to make their noses smaller and straighter, even dye their hair blonde. I don't do that, but, yeah, the British-sounding name would be part of all that. I'm also a proud member of Jewish Voice for Peace, we're pro-Palestinian and anti-bigotry in general."

"Cool. I had a Jewish guy once. He told me Jewish men were the best lovers."

"Ha, I bet he did."

"Seemed to me pretty much like the others. As usual with human men, I had to do most of the work."

"What do you mean?"

"Well, I'm a lot stronger than humans, so if I want to change position or something, I just flip them around."

I giggle. "They ever have a problem with that?"

"I'd say they never have a problem with anything as long as we're having sex," Evelyn says.

I giggle some more. "And how about mermen like Malcolm?"

She clams up with a knowing smile. "Oh, he's strong, like I am." Wink.

"So, are sex and eating, like, your biggest hobbies?" I ask in a chatty way.

"Yeah, well, now I'm into writing poetry, too."

"Hmm, sex, eating, and writing are my hobbies, too. Also, now cross-species gossip." I wink back.

"Well," Evelyn confides, "now I'm also forced to do some eco-stuff."

"Really, who's forcing you?"

"Survival! I'll tell you: This idiot Canadian company Enbridge Energy has run an oil pipeline underneath the Straits of Mackinac. It was only supposed to last 50 years, but now it's over 70 years old and looks like it's getting ready to burst in several spots. The mammoth oil spill that would result would be a disaster, horrible for us, for fish, for humans. Disgusting. Did you know that 1/3 of all Canadian humans and 1 in 10 American humans get their drinking water from the Great Lakes?! Michigan governor Whitmer has ordered a halt to the pipeline, but Enbridge is ignoring her and has started various harassment lawsuits, international law, US–Canadian border stuff, blah blah blah. Meanwhile, it's a horrible disaster waiting to happen. Now the company is saying they'll build a tunnel under the Lake and nearby lands to house a redirected pipeline, but they don't know what they're talking about. Some are saying their design is a pipe bomb waiting to happen. Recently, twelve tribes of Native Americans, along with Canadian First Nation activists, sent representatives to a UN meeting in Switzerland. One of them is the Bad River Band. In fact, part of the proposed tunnel would be right through the Bad River reservation, which is illegal. The Bad River Band is fighting back. We mer-people decided working with—or in parallel with—the tribes is our best bet. That's why I was so excited to meet Tim Moder's daughter at the READINGS event. X Moder, X is her activist name."

"Oh! I thought you were trying to flirt with Tim."

"Well, naturally, but I focused most on his daughter and her activism. I want to swim up to Superior and meet with her, get her advice."

"Evelyn, this is fantastic."

"Well, it's either diplomacy, which is like coalition-politics work, or packing fake seaweed work. My mer-group requires us to do one or the other." (She rolls her eyes.) "There's a bunch of mer-people who are wrapping the ancient pipeline with imitation seaweed, but that's only a temporary thing. I'd rather hang out in bars talking with human activists than wrap smelly sea grass."

"So, what concretely can you do to help out the Bad River Band efforts?"

"Oh, we're going to contribute to their legal fund. You want to chip in?"

"Well, I don't really have money. I'm retired. I could sign some petitions and stuff."

"What you could do is fence some jewelry for me!"

"You mean stolen jewelry?"

"Yep. I prefer to call it new-to-me jewelry."

"Evelyn, I'm *not* going to fence or pawn or whatever stolen goods."

"Why not?"

"If I get caught, I'd go to prison. Prisons in the US are very bad. No privacy, noisy, sometimes violent. Also, I like to stay up late and sleep late and they don't let you do that in prison. Then, too, I wouldn't get to play with Bruce hardly at all and that would make me sad. Wait a minute," I add, "you can't get Tim's daughter in trouble!"

"No worries, she has no idea where the money's coming from. I told her I was a rich poet."

"There is no such thing as a rich poet, Evelyn. You better come up with a better story. In fact, please don't involve her with stolen goods or profits from them at all! And where do you steal the jewelry from anyway?" I ask, holding on to my necklace.

"Oh, relax, that's gold plated not solid gold anyway, I can tell." She smiles.

Evelyn continues, "In the past, I took the jewelry from the different guys I met on the beach, mainly. I have such a good collection of gold wedding rings already." Big smile.

"OMG." (I don't think I'm getting the whole story here, but probably as much as I want to know.) "We have to think about this. Mainly I don't want to get Tim's daughter in trouble. I wish I knew more about money laundering, that way we could make sure any money you donate is squeaky clean."

"And, ahem, ahem, you're not worried I'll get caught?"

"Evelyn, I don't think any humans could catch you, unless you wanted us to."

"Haha, OK, we'll put our heads together on the money laundering. Should I ask X, Tim's daughter, too? For some money laundering ideas?" She arches her eyebrow.

"Absolutely not! Keep her completely out of anything illegal."

Evelyn giggles.

Episode 9
Evelyn and Maud Consider a Life of Crime

I'm at home, minding my own business, doing some of my editing work, thinking about the small flat white that will be mine at the café as soon as I get up there, when I check my email. An email from coolerthanhumans@mermail.com has come in. It says:

You know who this is. Let's meet same time, same day, same place next week. Don't email me back. I hate email and am hardly ever at the spa to check it anyway. Just show up. Or else.

That Evelyn. OK, sure, why not.

I'm there, with flat whites for Evelyn and me.

"Thanks, little human, this is delicious. OK, brass tacks," she starts. I see Evelyn has cut her hair short, and, on top of two seaweed helmets, she's wearing a fedora.

I interrupt, "Evelyn are you going all in on the Chicago gangster look?"

"Of course, dollface. Now, where was I? Yeah, you were right about the money laundering—it's illegal. Fines and jailtime if you're caught. We might have to go legit," she says.

"You have my attention."

"Buuuut, before we do."

"Uh oh."

"So, I looked you up. You used to work at the School of the Art Institute, right?"

"Yep."

"And you are a known associate of one Zach Cahill, an artist and writer at the University of Chicago, right?"

"True."

"So, you know something about the art world, see?"

"Well, some stuff . . . ," I say warily.

"Look here," says Evelyn, "do you want a knuckle sandwich?"

"Hon, threatening me with violence is not going to get you far," I say in my sternest voice. I'm a Scorpio, not to mention a former teacher. I bare my teeth at her.

"Jeezus K. Whilikers. I mean, cripes. It was just a figure of speech. Anyway, I read that art galleries are great for money laundering."

"I'm all ears."

"So, something like this. We get Zach to offer one of his paintings for sale at a friendly (she winks) gallery. We buy the painting for twice what it's selling for, we tell the gallerist it's for a good cause. Then the gallerist gives half the money to X Moder for the anti–Line 5 Pipeline Clean Lakes legal fund (or whatever they call it), takes a percentage from the listed price, and gives the rest of the money to Zach. We get the painting."

"I want the painting."

"No way, I'm taking it for the spa e-book reading room."

"Nope, too humid. I'm keeping the painting." I bare my teeth at Evelyn again.

"All right, all right, you have to stop doing that, though. It's not a good look."

I do it once more for good measure.

"You're lucky I'm still sipping my flat white."

I laugh.

We both sip and think. "Hmm, I like the plan except," I caution, "now Zach, the gallerist, X, you, and me are all involved in criminal activity and potentially face jail time and fines."

"Rats."

"Well, I have a plan that's only slightly fraudulent but not illegal."

"Can I still wear the fedora?" Evelyn asks.

"Yes."

"Here it is. We do a GoFundMe to fight the Line 5 Pipeline. Along with it, we have a website with the most gorgeous photos of Lake Michigan, Lake Huron, and Lake Superior topside, you know, delectable sunsets, rock formations, the works—to entertain and draw in our donors. And the real clinchers are the underwater photos—to be taken by you—of: (1) gorgeous underwater scenes like fish swimming and so forth and (2) exaggerated photos of the Line 5 Pipeline at points where it looks about to burst."

"What do you mean exaggerated?"

"Well, that's up to you. You can put make-up and paint on the pipeline to make it look even worse than it already does, use black paint to make it look like oil is leaking, that kind of thing."

"Gotta say, it already looks pretty bad in places already, but, yeah, I could exaggerate." Evelyn smiles.

I continue, "It's not exactly a lie, it's art. And it's not illegal, just . . . creative. Then we get the money and we give it to X for the legal fund."

"So, I get to be an artist? I think I'll dye my hair blue this time. Do you think I could get an art exhibition out of this?"

"Maybe, after we give the money to X and everything. I'll ask Zach."

Episode 10
Evelyn and Malcolm Go North

Hi, Maud! This is Evelyn, the email starts.

I'm sitting in the spa beneath the Crib near the Bad River Reservation of the Lake Superior Chippewa. The mer-people up here have done a VERY nice job on this spa. And yes, there are PAINTINGS on the walls. (Insert here whatever the fuck the emoji is for sticking the tongue out—I don't have time to look it up.)

Remember do NOT respond to this email. I don't know when I'll be at a spa next.

So, Malcolm and I met with X Moder. She's the bomb even if she is human (don't cry, you're OK, too). You're always talking about what people are wearing so I'll tell you. Malcolm and I, in order to dress up as human people, went through his collection of historical mer-people costumes used over the centuries when we have had to land. He has a background in the theater, did I tell you that? We found this fantastic 19th-century set, a grand lady's dress for me and a suit for him, but then Malcolm said we couldn't wear those to the meeting because humans who dressed like that, or the frontier version of that, were the ones who colonized Chippewa land. We might trigger intergenerational trauma (yes, he talks like that, but he's hot, so I go with it). Then we switched to clothes mer-people had designed themselves. A long, black velvet skirt and matching jacket for me. (I like wearing long skirts on land because I spark when I get excited and the velvet discreetly curtains the sparks.) Malcolm found black corduroy pants and a maroon corduroy shirt. I told him he couldn't wear the shirt because it was a different color from my outfit and he said I didn't get to make all the decisions, just most of them. Sigh.

We got to the bar-restaurant (you'd like it, it has tin ceilings like Printers Row Wine Bar), and X was wearing corduroy, too! Navy blue pants with a matching jacket. So, you see, we all matched more or less.

Turns out, X is very strict! We can't fake any of the photos for the raising-money website! It's not necessary anyway because the Bad River Band has drone images of the rapid erosion around the pipeline as it trespasses their land, erosion causing the pipeline to be at the mercy of the elements. And they have images of the 12,000-pound anchor that banged against it in 2018 on the Straits of Mackinac, and the resulting dent and coating peel, so you can see how easily the pipeline gets damaged. She said we could use those, and yes, she believes they'd welcome fund raising, as long as there are no tricks. (They already work with the Native American Rights Fund, narf.org, but she said the more the merrier.)

Turns out the Bad River Band has been in ferocious legal fights with Enbridge since 2019! They won a big case this year where the judge required Enbridge to get the pipeline off their land (or shut it down) and to give them over 5 million dollars. You might think, then why do we have to fundraise for them. Well, try to be far sighted, little human. Enbridge immediately appealed and tangled the whole thing up legally, so X thinks it might be a cold day in hell before they actually see that money. Meanwhile there are legal bills to pay. Plus recently (as we read in our research) they sent a representative along with ones from other tribes, led by Whitney Gravelle, president of the Bay Mills Indian Community, and ones from Canadian First Nation groups to Switzerland to lobby the UN for support in closing down Line 5 and saving drinking water for all animals and humans and everyone who uses the Great Lakes. They need to pay off that trip too. The UN agreed with them—and recommended that Line 5 be shut down! But so far, no dice. The Canadian government is especially unhelpful and devoted to Enbridge and money. Gravelle and Bay Mills's slogan is, You can't drink oil. She has a point. I'd like to meet her sometime.

X gave us some literature too. Did you know (this is from narf), "Line 5 has already leaked at least 33 times and discharged more than 1.1 million gallons of oil"?! Barf. Stupid fucking humans.

Once we get the site up and running, the Bad River Band will check it out and, if they like it, will let us say something like, With the approval of the Bad River Band. At this point, I was sparking a lot and some of the sparks were falling on my shoes. X said what's that. I said I was wearing special battery-powered, heat-producing stockings that sometimes sparked. She looked a little skeptical but let it go.

We told her we were citizen scientists and environmentalists, and she liked that. She asked what we did for a living, and I said we were retired. My hair was dyed black (like at the poetry reading), but Malcolm has some gray streaks showing in his hair. X said he looked a little like the Golden Bachelor, but smarter. We didn't know what that meant but nodded like we did. (Oh, I know, I know, it's a TV show, but I don't have time to watch TV.)

X asked how we got up there, and I said we swam. She laughed. She said no really. Malcolm jumped in and said we'll never tell (acting). We all sat around drinking beer and spinning stories. A lot of ours started out, Out on the Lake one day. I guess she thinks we do a lot of boating. And fishing. And possibly that we live near Lake Superior, not Lake Michigan. But it's best to be a little mysterious. We said you were going to be involved in the money-raising website too, and she remembered you from the reading and from your working with her dad, Tim.

Then X had to run. Malcolm and I swam to this spa where we spent the night, ate a lot of raw fish, drank coffee (they have a great coffee maker), and now we're getting ready to swim back home. We'd like to spend some more time up here, but we want to swim back before things start to freeze over. And yeah, we would've brought you along, but you can't swim this far, so shut up.

See you soon at the Point. Maybe you could wear a velvet outfit too, but don't wear maroon, OK? And maybe you could meet Malcolm sometime.

Or else, Evelyn

Episode 11
Evelyn, Maud, and the Guys Wrestle with Moral Dilemmas

Back in Chicago, and back on Promontory Point, it's late December, 36 fucking degrees out, Lake-effect snow is shimmering in the air, drifting down, and the gang is having a picnic. Bruce and Maud have brought Thai food, Malcolm and Evelyn have brought hot tea.

I smile at Malcolm who is, in fact, easy on the eyes. "It is so great to meet you, Malcolm!"

"A pleasure, Maud, you're looking very healthy."

Ah, another Midwestern mer-person. I beam back. I'm going to like this guy.

Bruce edges closer to me saying, "We'd better huddle together for warmth." I like it when he gets jealous.

Evelyn narrows her eyes at me, always a little scary when that happens. She says, "Let's eat before we have our meeting." I like her priorities.

I can't even figure out what they're wearing this time—layers of mysteriously dry puffer-wear and vintage seaweed gloves and hats. They seem more comfortable than Bruce and me in our usual single-layer down coats and wool hats.

"What's this?" asks Malcolm.

"Pad Thai with chicken, that's basil chicken, this is rice, that's cucumber salad," Bruce says.

"Dead birds," says Malcolm under his breath.

Bruce gives him a look, "If you don't want chicken you can eat the Pad Thai noodles with cucumber salad."

"Oh," Evelyn elbows Malcolm, "he'll eat just about anything, fish is his specialty, but he's omnivorous."

Bruce and I nod.

Evelyn continues, "He even ate some humans when he was younger."

This does not have the desired reassuring effect she may've been intending.

"Now, now, Evelyn," says Malcolm, "they were already dead." Turning to us, he explains, "They'd drowned in a boating accident. I merely wanted to see what they tasted like. And I didn't eat them, I nibbled." He adds proudly, "I think that was the beginning of developing my gourmet palate."

Bruce and I huddle even closer together.

"No worries," says Malcolm, "I'm a pacifist, except where fish are concerned." He smiles broadly, incisors showing.

"Alrighty then," I say, "maybe we could even start the meeting while we're eating since it's so cold out."

"OK, little human," says Evelyn, "well"—dramatic pause—"we have some moral quandaries due to some things we learned on our trip."

"Oh, maybe Bruce can help with those, he's very moral, me not so much," I respond, also smiling.

"So, here's the deal," Evelyn sits up straighter. "Recently the Bad River Band asked for an emergency injunction against Enbridge to shut down the pipeline because part of Line 5 on their land (illegally!, asshole Enbridge) is near two banks on a Bad River meander that's eroding fast, exposing more and more of the pipeline, and increasing the danger of a rupture. The judge, William Conley, said the tribe needs to play nice with Enbridge and allow the company to shore up the bank at that point. The tribe says no, Enbridge is there illegally and has to take the pipeline out, preferably shutting it down altogether. Judge Conley refuses to grant the emergency halt."

Malcolm arranges himself in some sort of Zen pose during

this story, legs crossed and hands in a prayer position, his eyes closed.

Evelyn does a little eye roll, whispers to me, "That's his conflict resolution pose." She continues, "So, while we admire the tribe's hard line, we're worried that oil might leak at that juncture. We're thinking we or some mer-people living up there might swim in and shore up (get it?) those banks, while the conflict is going on. I mean, we live in these waters and don't want any oil pollution, or more than is already there."

Bruce asks, "How likely is it that there would be breakage there over the winter?"

Evelyn sighs, "Yeah, not a bad question for a human. The ground will freeze and the banks should hold fine till spring, that's when we have to worry, especially with the climate-change increase in rainfall."

"OK," Bruce responds, "why not leave it alone for now and talk more to X, so you're not going behind the Bad River Band's back. In my opinion, you're allied with them now and need to respect what they're doing."

Malcolm opens his eyes, "Hey, are you one of those sensitive men?"

"Well, I don't know about that," Bruce says, looking tough.

"I think it's a compliment," I quickly say. "Malcolm, did you know that Bruce is a tap dancer?"

"Really! I'm part of a mermen's group that does something like that except we call it tail thumping."

Evelyn laughs, "I know something else I'd call tail thumping." Some mer-wrestling ensues, although the layers stay on. Bruce and I watch for a while, then keep eating. They come up for air.

The tip of my nose is freezing. I'm rubbing it. "Would you like me to warm up your nose for you?" asks Malcolm, "I can breathe on it." He smiles and I can see his incisors again.

"No thanks," Bruce answers for me, putting his arm around me and pulling me closer. Bruce changes the subject. "Was there another moral quandary?"

"Well," says Evelyn, hesitantly. (I've never seen her hesitate before.) "You know this money we're going to raise? We've been wanting an espresso machine for our spa. We were wondering if we could skim a little off the top since we're working so hard and everything."

"No," say Bruce and I together.

"You know we're bigger than you," says Evelyn. Bruce gives her a look, and it's not one I have to worry about. To think I was ever worried about those two.

I say, "Well, Bruce is a comptroller in his day job, and he can tell you that for tax purposes we have to account for the money we raise and give all of it to the Bad River Band's nonprofit."

Evelyn shrugs like she couldn't care less. "Oh, it's only money, we'll get it some other way." She winks at Malcolm.

I don't ask.

Episode 12
Evelyn Plans

From: coolerthanhumans@mermail.com
To: justmaud@poetmail.com
Cc: eatitraw@mermail.com

Maud, while we're grateful for your and Bruce's two cents, Malcolm and I have decided to go our own way on this. Still, I think our plans will warm your little tiny human hearts. Just to let you know:

We've decided to hold off on the website raising funds for Bad River Band's legal work until next spring. Enbridge is delaying things with its appeal anyway. What we aim to do after the worst of winter is to underwater-photograph the entire pipeline so we can montage the images together online and make a splash, haha. We also want to monitor what is happening with Line 5 inch by inch. We're particularly concerned about the Line in the Straights of Mackinac. Our fake-seaweed packing is ongoing—being done mostly by the Upper Peninsula mcr-people at present, mainly in this area.

We're going to leave the part of Line 5 trespassing the Bad River reservation alone, following the tribe's wishes, but will continue to monitor it, too. I bet the tribe is doing the same.

OK, lil human, deal with it. We have a lot at stake here!

Or else, Evelyn

Ps—Malcolm insists I add this postscript. We semi-hibernate over the winter deep in the Lake. Never you mind where. But we come topside once in a while. Malcolm would like to see you and Bruce (I wouldn't mind either). He says we could change into legs and come see Bruce perform some tap thumping. I could do a poem. So could you. Malcolm will bring some raw fish stew, if you want. Let us know.

From: justmaud@poetmail.com, tapbruce@taptaptap.com
To: coolerthanhumans@mermail.com, eatitraw@mermail.com

Evelyn and Malcolm, thank you for your gracious email. We can't wait to see the photomontage of the entire pipeline. And yeah, we think waiting till spring for the website is OK. You've already conferred with X Moder, yes? Even though she's a human, you need to weigh in her wishes, natch. (Yes, I can be bossy, too.)

We'd love to invite you to watch Bruce tap in collaboration with our friend Calvin Forbes reading some poetry at one of writer Westley Heine's readings nights at Gallery Cabaret. Most of the evening is open mic, and you and I could each read a poem!

xxoo, Very Human Maud

Episode 13
Gallery Cabaret, End of November

Gallery Cabaret is up near Bucktown, with a long, wooden floor, round plastic tables, a bar on one side, and a raised wooden stage at one end. Poet Westley Heine, a generation or more younger than Bruce and me, has participated in one of my READINGS events at Printers Row Wine. I don't know how and I don't know why, but Westley is a beatnik. He hasn't had an easy life, but along the way he's written some great stuff and gotten literary circles going in all kinds of places, mainly bars, some beaches. He's a Chicago treasure. And a friendly one.

Bruce and I are sitting at a table up front and to the side with Calvin Forbes, a handsome gent and eminence grise of the poetry world, a good friend and one of my favorite poets anywhere, and his partner Jin Lee, an artist and photographer, also a good friend. Calvin and Bruce have their heads together, going over their tap/poetry collaboration. Bruce's head is shaved, his blue shirt untucked, his pants loose, his tap shoes Kelly green. He is, as always, a snack and a half. Jin and I are sitting back sipping and gossiping, glad not to be in the spotlight for once.

In walk Evelyn and Malcolm! Each in all black, with black berets. Once again, I'm struck by how tall they are, Evelyn is what, about 6'2", Malcolm I'd put at about 6'4". Evelyn is wearing a black velvet skirt and velvet top, and Malcolm is also in black velvet this time, flowing shirt and pants. They're carrying their black puffer jackets, which have a faint glow about them.

"Hi!" I can't believe they came, especially as they didn't answer my last email. "Hi!" Evelyn swoops in with a cheek kiss for me and a hand wave at Bruce. Malcolm smiles and nods serenely. They're not wearing masks this time because it's been discovered that mer-people can't get Covid, but Bruce and I are wearing ours, and Calvin and Jin have theirs handy, I guess in case the place starts filling up.

I make the introductions. Calvin assesses. I say, "Um, we met Evelyn and Malcolm through some eco stuff to do with Lake Michigan, and Evelyn read at Printers Row Wine, she's a poet." (Calvin has also read at Printers Row Wine.) Evelyn's hair remains short, now a kind of iridescent green. Malcolm has kept his salt-and-pepper look.

"What eco stuff?" asks Jin.

Uh oh, I forgot she's an eco-activist. "Oh, well, just some stuff at 57th Street beach," I dodge, "and we might work together to raise some money for the Bad River Chippewa tribe in northern Wisconsin and their long legal battle against Enbridge and Line 5." Jin nods knowingly, she's up to date on Line 5.

Calvin looks at Evelyn. "You're tall," he says. Calvin is heterosexual. He has his own sparks, if you know what I mean.

Jin shakes her head. "Have a seat," she says, "grab a few chairs." She looks at Evelyn and points to the space between me and her. Malcolm pulls up the chairs, and they both squeeze into the space. I see a crockpot-looking thing he's brought with him, letting off a slight fishy smell.

"Oh," I rush, "I don't think we're allowed to bring outside food in here."

Malcolm puts it under his seat. "No problem, more for Evelyn and me later." He smiles benignly.

Westley warms up the modest crowd. "Hey, man, so cool you're here," he says to the audience. Effusively, he introduces Calvin and Bruce. They deserve every glowing word. And then they're up on stage and going. Calvin reads his latest poem, Bruce taps along with intricate choreography. It's beautiful.

They really listen to each other and somehow share a beat as well as leave room for Bruce's improv tangents. You can tell they're friends and respect each other. I give Evelyn a side glance and she's rapt. Good. I'm not in the mood for bratitude tonight. Then, surprise, Calvin and Bruce do one more poem and tap duet. I didn't know they were going to do a second one. This one is lighter, springier, but still gripping. I love both numbers.

A lot of applause, and Westley moves into the open mic portion. "Who wants to read tonight? We'll start with one poem each." Evelyn and I raise our hands, so do about eight others, mostly men, around the tables. "OK, let's start with the ladies." Evelyn strides up. She takes the mic. Westley sits down in the audience. Evelyn goes strong:

"Go Fuck Yourself

I want you like I've never wanted anyone.
Not the guy on the beach, or that other guy on the beach.
Or, yeah, any of them.
But if you tell me to meditate one more time,
I'll tell you to
Go Fuck Yourself!"

(I'm thinking, is there trouble in paradise? Too much closeness in partial hibernation? Evelyn continues.)

"Shut up, I want you.
You are so fucking sexy."

There's a lot of applause. Malcolm stands up, Evelyn leaps off the stage, lands next to him, they embrace. And nuzzle.

"Get a room!" someone in the crowd yells.

Malcolm sits Evelyn and himself down with a stage whisper, "Later, babe."

Oh, rats, I have to go next. How can I follow that?

I look in my phone at a few poems. I decide to counter with sweetness and gratitude, a poem I wrote for Bruce:

"Ladybug: A Love Poem with Sliced Fruit and Cocoa Powder
[Copihue Poetry, Summer 2023]

I could write about your ass, spherical
    Your smooth skin, your scent
    Your voice, your accent with twang
    Your laugh, easy and sharp.

It's more than that, you know
    I can exist with you, all good.
    I'm eating a late-night snack, and
    You tell me I'm beautiful.
    I stay up into the wee hours and
    Sleep late whenever I can, and
    You say I work hard.
    I put cocoa powder on my sliced fruit
    Getting it everywhere, and
    You say do we need to order more.
    I stick rhinestones above my brow
    With eyelash glue, and
    You say you like how the light shines.

Thank you, darlin', with you,
    I feel like a ladybug, bringing good luck
    Just by being here."

I sit back down, Bruce squeezes my hand under the table. Calvin feigns wiping the sweat off his brow. Jin smiles. Evelyn gives me a wink.

Westley is back on stage. "OK, guys, eat your Wheaties, you got some competition."

I squeeze Bruce's hand, look knowingly at him, smile at Jin, smile at Calvin. And give Evelyn a wink back.

Episode 14
Maud in a Pickle at AWP

Sure enough, we didn't see Evelyn and Malcolm for a while in the winter, although Evelyn and I emailed. Then it was February, and we did, or I did, and then some. I'll tell you about it.

I'd been looking forward to the AWP, Association of Writers & Writing Programs, conference in Kansas City for months. Months! Couldn't decide whether to fly down from Chicago or to take Amtrak. Ended up taking Amtrak even though it's a 7 hour and 10 minute ride. Why? Evelyn and Malcolm, who for reasons unclear to me decided they also wanted to go to AWP, don't like to fly. They'd tried it once decades ago and said never again. The seats were too small, no raw fish was served for snacks. When the plane took off, Evelyn had sparked, and there were questions. Long story short, we ended up taking the train.

Certain parties complained a lot on the train. It was too hot. The windows were stuck (finally Malcolm yanked one out of its frame when no one was looking). The snack bar ran out of M&Ms. Walking up and down the aisles didn't give them the relief it gave me because they really didn't like using their legs that much. And that's only the tip of the iceberg.

Then there was the argument at the hotel in Kansas City. We were supposed to have two rooms, one for me (Bruce was back in Chicago, working) and one for them. Turns out, they never made their reservation, figuring all three of us could share my room. I put my foot down.

"Absolutely not, you guys, I'm a light sleeper and I really need my sleep to hit all the panels and off-site readings. Get your own room."

There was a certain amount of pushing and shoving. I held my ground even though they're much taller and stronger than me. I really like to get a good night's sleep. Finally, they were able to get their own room at the last moment even though the hotel had been sold out, due to a cancellation. And thank God, it was nowhere near mine.

The desk clerk said to me, "Is that Taylor Swift and Travis Kelce in disguise?" looking over at their tallnesses (6'2" and 6'4").

"Please don't tell the paparazzi," I whispered.

She said, "But why are they staying here—don't they have a house in KC?"

"Security reasons," I replied.

This gave me an idea. I went up to Evelyn and Malcolm's room to help them settle in. They started arguing over which one of them would get to spend the night in the bathtub.

"Guys, guys, you know what would be a good trick to play on humans in Kansas City?" They looked interested. "Evelyn, all you have to do is buy a blond wig, find one that's a bit brownish-blond, not too brassy or bleached looking, shoulder-length. Malcolm, all you have to do is buy a Kansas City Chiefs scarf. Otherwise wear your black coats and hats. Add some sunglasses. Walk around together holding hands and looking like you don't want to be recognized. Evelyn, look down a little, Malcolm, stride slightly ahead. You'll be taken for Taylor and Travis. When people recognize you, deny it, that'll make them sure you really are Taylor and Travis. They might even give you some free things. Tell me about it tomorrow. I'm off to take a nap. Oh, but please stay in the neighborhood of the hotel, don't go too far." And I was out of there.

I was able to wander around the book fair part of the conference that evening, undisturbed, and even to run into a few of my favorite authors in person like poet Taylor Byas. Slept late the next morning, skipping the panel "Is Your Book Hybrid or Did You Just Sneak a Few Poems in There," with zero guilt. Such a relief to sleep well, since I was going to be in an off-site reading that evening co-organized by LKE Editions and *Roi Fainéant*. I was very excited about it and wanted to shine my best. Goth princess from Mississippi, the sparkling Exodus Oktavia Brownlow, was in the same reading. I'd reviewed a couple of her books for *Reckon Review* but never met her in person. For that matter, a couple of the cool editors from *RF* were going to be there and I'd never met them in person either.

I caught one panel that afternoon, "How to Write Fantasy When Fantasy Is Really Your Reality," and let's just say it hit home. In the privacy of my room, I changed into my writer clothes for the evening, possibly inspired by Evelyn's fashion sense, a maxi-length black velvet skirt and loose top, made up my face with rhinestones, and added lots of barrettes with rhinestones to my hairdo. I was set.

The off-site was only one block away, ah, what luck, and no ice on the sidewalk, again lucky for mid-February. I got there early and there was Exodus, also early. She is the queen of dressing up for readings, or even just to run an errand, and she was wearing a goth black corset over a flowered ball gown, with bejeweled hair in luxurious curls piled atop her head. I didn't have to worry about what to say to her because we talked about how she made every element of her outfit. She said how her jewels and my rhinestones matched. I was flattered. Before I knew it, the reading had started. Exodus was slotted for last since she was more or less the star of the event, I was third to go. I threw myself into my reading and was pleased with it. Good applause at the end.

Then I heard, "Go, Maud, you're a deep dive into Lake Michigan and an even deeper one into Lake Superior!" yelled by two very tall people in the back. "Deep dive, deep dive," they boomed. It was nighttime but they were wearing sunglasses, and one had long blonde hair. The other wore a number 87 football jersey. They each had about twenty friendship bracelets on. Laughter broke out.

Exodus leaned over, "Are those sparks?"

I shrugged. "Those are my friends from Chicago, they might have been drinking some."

"You think?" said Exodus.

Evelyn and Malcolm were making little bows to the crowd. It seemed they were a hit.

There was a brief intermission. I rushed to the back and whispered, "You guys have to be super quiet and well behaved, don't interrupt the other readers, especially not Exodus at the end, I'm a fan."

"Please," Malcolm said, holding his gloved fingers in the lotus position to show he was Zen.

Evelyn said she wanted to read her "Eat It Raw" poem. I admitted I really like that poem but told her she couldn't read it, as the schedule was all planned way in advance and people had traveled to be here tonight to read. She pouted but then said fine, and convinced Malcolm to go back outside to walk the sidewalks together pretending to be Taylor and Travis. On the way out, she showed me the gleaming tennis bracelet a fan gave her that afternoon. I said, "I hope that's costume jewelry," she said she hopes it's diamonds.

"Bye for now," I said, "let's go to panels together tomorrow afternoon."

"Yeah, sure." Evelyn winked, waving bye.

"See you at 1:00 at the front desk."

That day ended pickle-free, thank goodness.

Episode 15
One More Winter Adventure, and a Twist

Evelyn, Malcolm, and I had made it back to Chicago by train with no further incidents, no more popped-out-of-their-frames windows. We had even hit a couple of panels together at AWP before leaving, "Is Fantasy the New Reality?" and "I'll Go to Any Panel Alexander Chee Is In," and had been happy (Maud) or bored (Evelyn) or meditating (Malcolm) during each. Heading home, Evelyn and Malcolm were in good moods from all their times on KC sidewalks being mistaken for Taylor and Travis and the loot they'd received. They even got me a black beret to match theirs. I wore it proudly on the train.

At the beginning of March, I get an invitation from my friend Zach to the opening of his one-person show at Ruschman Gallery in honor of Zach's new word-and-image book *Unicorn Death Moon*. The exhibition would include original pen-and-ink portraits of unicorns from the book and more artworks along the same theme. Excited, I plan again to wear my silver mermaid tights and a long black sweatshirt with, natch, my black beret. I've invited Evelyn, Malcolm, and their berets to go with Bruce and me to the opening. Bruce refuses to wear a matching beret, but then life is not something that can be controlled even at the best of times. And Bruce can't be controlled at any time (he is handsome though).

We all meet up at the gallery opening night. Zach is wearing his trademark pink woolen hat and his wife Holly is sporting one, too! I give a pointed look at Holly's hat, at Zach's hat, and then at Bruce, but Bruce, an evenhanded Libra, is more or less impervious to my Scorpio glare. Zach is also wearing pink sneakers, and he and Bruce, who is in black sneakers with yellow accents, launch into one of their conversations devoted to running and running shoes.

I cruise around the show with Evelyn and Malcolm. Need I say those two were both in black velvet? Evelyn is telling Malcolm that when she was a mer-girl, she'd ridden a unicorn once.

"You're kidding," says Malcolm, "I always wanted to meet one."

"Yep, this was in the Upper Peninsula, they used to live there till the humans overpopulated it. Then the unicorns moved north into Canada, north of the heavily populated zone near the US border, and up into the north central plains. Good thing they did, the waters bordering the UP have been taken over by invasive mussel species, and you know unicorns have sensitive feet, they wouldn't have liked that at all, those sharp shells. And they love to frolic at the water's edge."

"Unicorns are really real?!" I say.

"Oh, yeah," Evelyn replies, "but they don't like humans. They tolerate mer-people sometimes," she adds.

"Are they magic? Are they like fairies? Do they grant wishes?"

Evelyn looks serious. "I promised not to tell. Why don't you ask your friend Zach? Looks like he may be in touch with a few. Is he Canadian? He's tall. Maybe some of them met him up in Canada and thought he was mer-folk."

Zach is working the crowd though, so I make a mental note to ask him another time. He isn't Canadian, but I never know what Zach and Holly get up to on their vacations.

Suddenly, Evelyn's, Malcolm's, and my cellphones all ping at once. It's X Moder with a surprise announcement. The email is diplomatically worded but the gist of it is that she'd brought up our proposal for an anti-Enbridge, anti–Line 5 pipeline web site plus photography to fundraise for the tribe's lawsuits at a tribal meeting, and the tribe had said NO. Bad River Band of Lake Superior Chippewas felt there were already numerous websites about Line 5, and, further, any fundraising related to Line 5 trespassing on their land should be done directly by them. They also felt that as much as they appreciated the offer to underwater-photograph all of Line 5's travel through Lake Michigan, they didn't want that posted in case some saboteur used the information. X pointed out that the US government has a lot of enemies from sticking their noses and military might where it doesn't belong, and the last thing they wanted to do was to show a potential saboteur more Line 5 weak spots that would impact such a key source of drinking water. The tribe felt they'd suffered enough from the US government and its "friends" already.

X, also a Midwesterner, added that she'd love to see Evelyn and Malcolm again next time they were up her way and she'd enjoyed hanging out with them.

All in all, a shocking turn of events.

Episode 16
A Few Days Later

Evelyn insists we all meet up on Promontory Point to be melodramatic, share our despair, and regroup.

The skies are gray, the Lake offers choppy waves, the stones are still icy, the wind is sharp. In fact, it is freezing out. After some general complaining that we'd been looking forward to working with the Bad River Band (not that they'd asked us to), a consensus forms among Evelyn, Malcolm, Bruce, and me that we can see X Moder's point and that interference in Native American business had not worked out well historically for them, so we have to, in Malcolm's words, stop thinking like colonizers. And we all understand we can still keep following the different groups, Chippewa and non, and websites [please see Appendix] already fighting for Line 5's closure, and offer support when general public action is called for. Plus, different mer-groups are going to continue monitoring Line 5 across its journey in and near the Lake.

I point out there are other threats to the Lake that we could work on, and everyone nods at that, too.

Evelyn adds though, "But I wanted to play with the cool kids! And the Bad River Band is so cool."

"Maybe we could give X a beret?" I say. "Also if you keep coming to the wine bar, Tim Moder will come down again at some point to read his poetry and you know he's cool."

Evelyn sulks. "Yeah but I can't play too much with him 'cause I'm with Malcolm now." (Malcolm looks heavenward.)

"Tim isn't a toy!" I say protectively. "He's a poet. You could talk poetry with him."

It's at this moment that Malcolm suggests he and Bruce go to the Promontory Point Fieldhouse. Bruce can show him some tap steps, and he can show Bruce some tail thumping moves (the dance kind). We watch them head off. I'd thought the Fieldhouse was locked, but can see at a distance Malcolm doing something to one of the doors, and then they're inside.

Evelyn leans forward. "I'll tell you what's really upsetting me. Like I said, in our mer-group we have the choice to either do diplomacy or to wrap imitation seaweed around the trouble spots in Line 5. Now that I've failed at the diplomatic mission, I'll have to wrap sea grass. (A) It's really boring and slow. (B) It's not even seaweed since the invasive mussel species ate all the seaweed in the Great Lakes, and what's left is this imitation seaweed called *Cladophora* which stinks to high heaven. Is it just me," she adds, "or does *Cladophora* sound like venereal disease? I miss seaweed. The seaweed helmets we wear are vintage. The smelly stuff is what's left now. I refuse to work with it."

"OK, I get it. But, here's some cheerful news . . . I've been Googling around, and . . . drumroll . . . I think we could work on lessening agricultural runoff in Lake Michigan!" I beam at her.

"Does that sound exciting to you?" Evelyn narrows her eyes at me.

I narrow mine back. "Listen, Evelyn, I grew up in Canton, Ohio, actually outside Canton, on an unpaved road where so little happened that my brothers and I used to count the number of cars that went by in an afternoon to entertain ourselves. There weren't many. So, yes, it sounds exciting to me."

"You had a boring childhood."

"Yep, at times. But it was also pretty there with marshlands and corn fields. And, well, we learned to make our own fun, making up stories, exploring the marsh. So, I think we can make this agrarian runoff thing fun. Truth to tell, I've already been thinking about it some."

I clear my throat and continue, "At first I was thinking we could involve 4-Hers in Michigan. The Michigan Farm Bureau together with 4-H has yearly Excellence in Agriculture Awards and we could get some of those awardee kids involved in stopping nitrate and phosphorous runoff, or slowing it! You know, I was in 4-H as a kid."

"What's 4-H?"

"What's 4-H?! What's 4-H?!!!" I sigh. "It's mainly rural clubs across the country for kids where they raise livestock or sew or learn new technologies. And then each club shows annually at county fairs. Kind of like Future Farmers of America. I was in a 4-H sewing club for years during grade school. The 4-H motto is 'Head, Heart, Hand, and Health: I pledge my head to clearer thinking, my heart to greater loyalty, my hands to larger service, and my health to better living, for my club, my community, my country, and my world.'"

"Maud, this explains a lot."

"Yes, it does," I say, chin out, shoulders back. "Your sarcasm is not appreciated. You're probably just jealous."

"Well, I was in the Little Mermaids."

"Oh, that sounds cute. What did you do?"

"We got a medal every time we tipped over a human boat."

"Whoa, isn't that dangerous? Even deadly?"

"Oh, relax, we had to promise not to kill or permanently injure any humans."

"Did you, um, keep that promise?"

"What?" Evelyn had a faraway look in her eyes. "Oh, yeah, more or less."

My Scorpio stare is back.

"Haha, no worries, I'm a pacifist now."

"Somehow, I doubt it. Evelyn, are you paying attention?"

"Uh, yeah, sure, we're going to do diplomacy with 4-H kids."

"Well, I admit, that was my first thought. But then I remembered you can't, as a stranger, just approach a kid and ask them to work with you—there's all kinds of laws protecting kids from child predators. Not that we're child predators, but we are adults. So, I don't think we can contact the prize winners individually, even though their names are publicly announced. And if we go through the 4-H club bureaucracy, it might take forever."

"So?"

"I'm working on an idea about 4-H alumni! We 4-H alumni and friends could get together and do something, and you could participate and count that as your diplomacy."

"Anything to get out of working with that smelly imitation seaweed. Yeah, maybe. Now that you mention it, less farm runoff would mean fewer giant algae blooms in the Lake and some of that really stinks, too, and some is even toxic. So, yeah, I'm in."

"Give me time to think about this."

Episode 17
Maud Talks About It in Therapy

A while back, I'd admitted to my therapist Michele that my new friend Evelyn was a mermaid. Michele did a small double take, but quickly collected herself, and asked, "Who do you think Evelyn represents?"

I could tell she thought I was making Evelyn up. Little did she know. I didn't protest though because I wasn't supposed to tell anyone about Evelyn being a mermaid besides Bruce.

Today I'm telling Michele how ambivalent I felt about getting 4-H alumni together to help farmers eco-improve their farms. Not keen on organizational work. From the research I'd been doing on farmland.org and other places, it seems like many farmers are already for environmental goals intertwined with protecting the soil and maximizing the bottom line, but it costs money to, say, lessen phosphorous runoff and states tend to only partially fund these efforts. Seems like a group that would welcome fundraising and labor assistance, in conjunction with their leadership. Or at least some farmers would.

On the other hand, fundraising and labor assistance sounds like kind of a drag. I mean, I already have back problems, and helping to plant a, say, clover border to contain some runoff around acres of farmland does not sound like it'd be good for my back. Also, I'm not a seasoned fundraiser nor knowledgeable about farming. Raising money for organic mulch cover sounds like an uphill climb. Not as sexy as fighting a big oil company. And the potential administrative work is a red flag. I had to do admin work at my last job, and didn't like it.

Maybe I'm just lazy?!

Michele urges me not to beat myself up. I, however, think being lazy is a commendable trait. It had long been a goal of mine to further develop that trait, before I retired, but work kept getting in the way.

"What do you like about Evelyn?" she asks.

"She's fun and she never does anything she doesn't want to do. She likes eating, sex, clothes, swimming, and writing, like I do."

"Well, could you bring some of those things into eco-work?"

"Hmm, good question. I need some time to think about that."

"Remember the old saw, try to be inspired by desire instead of obligation," says Michele.

She has a point.

Episode 18
Daydreams of a Person Aspiring to Be Lazy and an Eco-Freak at the Same Time

April is the spritziest month. I sit at the kitchen table looking out at the spritz and daydreaming.

What if, what if Bruce, Evelyn, Malcolm, and I owned a small farm in Southwest Michigan, somewhere inland from Saugatuck or Holland, you know, in the Douglas/Fennville area. On it would sit a small house for Bruce and me and a small spa for Evelyn and Malcolm when they're on land. It would be a blueberry farm and we could call it Sparkly Blueberries. In the summer, we could swim in Lake Michigan at Oval Beach whenever we wanted. And in the winter we could swim at the Aquatic Center in Holland.

We could hire people to work the farm and pay them ample, beyond-good wages.

We could eat in all the delicious cafés around there, whatever we want, and never gain weight.

There would be an educational and fundraising aspect of the farm, promoting organic farming. As far as I can figure, the goals are to increase nutrients in the soil and decrease agricultural runoff into streams and rivers—all needed in our immediate area and the larger Great Lakes watershed. These tactics also help farms in the event of extreme weather conditions like torrential rains, which are increasing during climate change. There's an array of practices like reducing tilling, diversifying crop rotations, and keeping "the soil covered with living or dead (mulch) vegetation at all times" (farmland.org).

There'd be an educational display spelling all this stuff out—in a fun way—and how this can be done economically. Otherwise, we'd be busy visiting cafés, swimming, writing, tap dancing, and going back to Chicago to see friends and do readings. Or, in Evelyn and Malcolm's case, swimming around Lake Michigan and Superior and leading gourmet food tours for mer-people. I'm loving this daydream.

The Sparkly Blueberries Farm would turn a profit. The profit would go back into the farm, with a little set aside for our old, old age.

What about startup funds?

We'd win the lottery (although we don't even play the lottery).

I have the dream, but I need some help.

Perhaps it's time to call another meeting with Evelyn and all, this time in a warm place.

Episode 19
Evelyn Hangs Out at
necessary & sufficient coffee

"I can't believe you're making us meet so far from the shore."

"Evelyn, we went to Kansas City together."

"Yeah, but this is Chicago. There's no excuse here hanging out anywhere too far from Lake Michigan."

"I'm not sitting my little human ass on those cold rocks at Promontory Point again till the temps rise."

Evelyn rolls her eyes.

Malcolm looks at her. "What's with you today, honey pot?"

"My legs are itching. I like my mermaid tail much better."

Malcolm gives her a kiss on the cheek.

We're sitting around a table at necessary and sufficient coffee in the South Loop, the four of us. It's a Saturday so Bruce is here, too. We've got lattes, banana bread, and delicious homemade soup made by Tropicake and sold at necessary. necessary coffee has not one, but two new air filters, high ceilings—14 feet, mind you—and a spacious layout. Kate, the owner, is into Covid safety, and S., who works there, is a writer. I love this place. Bruce does, too.

Now Bruce is looking with not-the-friendliest determination at Evelyn. "Sorry your legs itch," he says. "Try your latte," he adds firmly. "This is our favorite café in Chicago. Everything here is delicious."

Evelyn takes a sip of her latte, looks pleased, and starts to relax. Malcolm strokes her thigh in a comforting way.

"How's the tapping going, Bruce?" says Malcolm.

"Great, Calvin and I got another booking."

"Excellent, excellent, well, let us know when it is. We'd like to come, or I would."

"I would too." Evelyn beams at Bruce.

We settle in.

I share my daydream. Everyone likes the idea of being a lazy eco-activist and hanging out near Saugatuck. Turns out that Evelyn loves Oval Beach! "So do I," I say, "I love swimming there."

Now all we need is a small blueberry farm with all the trimmings.

Malcolm looks at Evelyn. Evelyn looks at Malcolm. Something is going on between them, but I can't tell what.

Malcolm wags his head from side to side in small movements, like he's signaling I don't know, I'm not sure.

Stalling for time, they turn the conversation to clothing. Not that I mind.

"Tell us about your color choices today, Maud," Malcolm says, in an obvious attempt at flattery. I love flattery.

"These are some vintage midnight blue velvet pants I had altered. I thought they'd look good with this buttercup yellow tunic sweatshirt. Bruce got his beautiful blue-and-beige tweed jacket this fall. We dressed up for you guys." I smile at him.

"No berets?"

"Well, they don't cover out ears so we went with wool pull-down hats today. And you?"

"Oh, we like to go with black velvets for getting together with you and Bruce since you're arty. This time matching maroon pants and tailored maroon tops."

"They have tailors underwater?" I ask.

"We have everything," Malcolm says, smiling gently.

Evelyn elbows him, and then gives him a nod.

He nods back and points to her.

"OK, we have something to tell you," Evelyn announces, sitting tall.

(Pause.)

"Someone we're friends with, he owns a small blueberry farm outside Fennville!"

"No way," I say.

"You're kidding." Bruce leans forward.

"No way," I say again.

Evelyn looks triumphant. She loves a dramatic reveal. Malcolm puts his arm around her and admits, "Truth to tell, we're the ones who encouraged him to make this investment a while back." He looks deeply satisfied.

"Brilliant," says Bruce.

I'm flabbergasted. "It's not, by any chance, a U Pick Em, is it?" I'd imagined that getting in a flow of people that way would be good for the educational arm of eco-farming.

"It sure is!" says Malcolm. "Although," he adds, "he might be moving away from that model since he's private and doesn't want too many strangers around."

"You know someone with a blueberry farm near Fennville? Are you pulling my leg? I still can't believe it."

"Nope, truth!"

"Wait a minute," I interject, "is it Gold Barn Blueberries or Wa-Hu Blueberry Farm or Fellinlove Farm? I've been studying those online."

"Nope."

"So, how did this happen?" asks Bruce.

"Well," says Malcolm, "our friend is a merman who for complex reasons likes to farm above water. It's a passion of his and he's even tackled the legal side."

"He has human-type ID and a bank account," Evelyn adds, "he has a driver's license and a social security number!" She lowers her voice. "We think he may've gotten the social security number from a dead baby!"

I lower mine, too. "Did he?! How? No, never mind, I don't want to know."

"Oh, I doubt he was involved in the baby's death," says Malcolm. "He's very careful with humans."

Malcolm changes the subject. "Maybe he'd let us contribute some eco-stuff to his already organic-leaning farm and put up an educational display. Who knows, maybe even add a little hut with an espresso machine for lattes." He cautions, "I'm afraid I can't tell you more till I confer with him. Mum's the word, meanwhile."

We all celebrate this possibility with extra lattes, decaf for this second round.

Bruce and I kiss. Evelyn says "Aw," and pats me on the head. It occurs to me they might regard us as pets.

Episode 21
Meeting Evelyn Again at necessary coffee

I'm already at the café with my spiral-bound notebook and flat white at a table away from other humans, basking in the filtered air and eating one of Tropicake's Filipino, ube mini-macaroons.

Evelyn sweeps in. I notice she's wearing the same black velvet skirt and top I've seen before, and think maybe she doesn't have as extensive a landlubber vintage wardrobe as she'd previously bragged. That's OK, I know what it's like to live on a budget too.

The sunlight and floor-to-ceiling windows show off the 19th-century red brick Printers Row façade across the street. I look up at Evelyn. "Hey, you're wearing glasses." I add, "Hmm, large black frames, no glass to speak of."

"They're for our meeting."

"Fetching."

"Did you get one of those for me?" She points at the flat white.

"No, get your own."

She picks up mine and takes a sip. "Hmm, not bad."

After she settles down with her own, I say, "You owe me a sip."

"As if," she replies.

I shoot her a look. "Let's get to work."

"OK, blueberry farming," she says in a new officious-sounding voice. "The merman farmer said yes, he's in for some eco-improvements and some educational materials, but he doesn't want an espresso shack down by the road. Too much of a bother running electricity and water down there. Since he doesn't really live in the house, plus already has a permit to serve non-alcoholic food there, he said we could have the front room and one bathroom. No one gets to go upstairs—that's where his spa is—or in the kitchen except to do dishes. Customers only in the front room."

"Well, that's very generous of him."

"Here's what we can sell: espresso, cappuccino, lattes, flat whites. No syrups except for his homemade blueberry syrup in the drinks. Or plain. Educational eco-materials have to be free. He wants us to sell some blueberries from the farm and some of his blueberry syrup. Keep it simple."

"That's all reasonable," I say, but wonder why she's barking out orders.

"Now," she continues, "with the educational materials, these are not mainly for other farmers who already know something about eco-farming, whether or not they're fully invested. They're for the tourists, especially those who vote in Michigan. We'll be coordinating with FLOW: For Love of Water and also Team Michigan LCV, Michigan League of Conservation Voters, to ask voters to support the legislation and candidates they're putting forward. And we'll give a little info on the eco-farming practices we're adding to the blueberry farm."

"What are those exactly?" (I guess she's done her research?)

"OK, I'm not an expert, but I think putting a border of clover or another sturdy ground cover around the perimeter of the farm to catch runoff is one way to help. Another really important one is when the early spring fertilizer is set out, we cover that with a light layer of mulch. For reasons I don't understand, this first dose of fertilizer is set out when the ground is still mainly frozen. Trouble is if there's heavy rain and it's not covered, it can wash right into the stream bordering the farm and then into the Lake. It has phosphorous in it which can cause imbalance in the Lake and algae blooms."

"What about the pesticides?"

"I have to do more research on that. Here's a piece of good news. I've been emailing some with X Moder, and it turns out her day job is doing advertising for agricultural companies. She said she could find out some more information."

"Malcolm and I would like you to run the store in the summer," she says in her lecturing voice.

I'm surprised but try to put my toe in for cooperation's sake. Still, why is she telling me what to do and not asking? "For the most part, I want to keep things lazy," I hedge. "I could maybe sit in the store, making the occasional latte and chatting up the customers. I don't want to clean the store, at least not deep clean it, I could redd up. Could we get some Little Mermaids to do some labor? Convince them it's for a badge or something?" I smile hopefully at Evelyn.

"Not sure," she says, "but great minds think alike. I was thinking of trying to rope them into planting the clover border around the farm."

I nod.

"Now, what about the merman farmer? Do we have to write up a report for him?"

"Well, you're the writer."

Ah. Well, isn't Evelyn free and easy about thinking up work for me to do all of a sudden. Where are Malcolm and Evelyn in these assignments? I wonder. And why am I the one who has to run this the whole summer?

Evelyn continues to explain in her bossy mode. "Here's the thing about that merman. He's a rebel. Being a land farmer is about as rebellious as you can get for a mer-person. What he really likes is not to be bothered. He'll give us a key. We have to have regular hours so he can avoid the foot traffic easily. And he wants to stay incognito. He likes the eco-stuff but we have to keep it in budget as what he makes from the farm already stretches for its maintenance, the harvesting, and so on. He even suggested we might want to do a drive for people in Fennville and Douglas to contribute mulch. He's willing to buy the clover, though, if we get it planted and keep it watered. He already pays someone a good living wage to come into the house to clean it once a week, and she can do the store too as long as we're not too slobby."

"How do you know we can count on his cooperation if he's so aloof?"

"Oh, I slept with him before I met Malcolm. He was fun but too much of a recluse for me—and there were other things. Actually, he won't be around much. He only hangs out at the farm when he's working or wants privacy. Otherwise, he's playing or swimming around the Lake. A real nature boy. I told him you and I are friends and all, but he says he may never meet you. He wants the farm to flourish and he likes eco-stuff—and his privacy most of all."

"Fine by me." I shrug. Curious already.

I'm not all that happy, though. I feel pressured, and have so many questions.

Episode 20
Maud Rebels

I've been thinking. My goal is to be a lazy activist. I like meeting friends at coffee shops, going to gallery shows, writing stories, doing readings, swimming in Lake Michigan, and playing with Bruce, with only a few surprises along the way. WTF is with this spending the summer at the mer-guy's house making lattes and chatting up Michigan voters, and who wants a hot latte when it's 90 degrees and humid anyway? And what's the point about being up in the Fennville–Douglas–Saugatuck area if I'm not at the beach? Where would I sleep? I don't have the money for an Airbnb or motel. I'm going to have to assert myself.

Time: a December day at dusk, 4:00 in the afternoon. Place: 57th Street beach. Attendees: Bruce, Evelyn, me.

I start. "Evelyn, I have to tell you I can't spend the summer making lattes at the mer-farmer's house."

Evelyn makes a big mistake—she pushes. "C'mon, Maud, where's your community spirit?! We have to save the Lake! Start this up right, we can set it up at other blueberry farms around Michigan." She's not listening to me.

She's so fucking arrogant, I think. I try to gather myself to speak. But I'm getting angry, I even start crying. Then I burst out.

"I DON'T WANT TO!!! I don't want to save the Lake, I want to SWIM in it. I don't want to make lattes, I want to sip iced tea. I want air conditioning! Where am I supposed to sleep? I don't want to sleep on the floor of the store! I don't want an absentee landlord who never appears and makes rules I have to follow! I don't like the smell of raw fish! I hate raw fish! I don't want to organize Little Mermaids! When I worked at my old job, I had to be departmental chair in addition to teaching. I had to be graduate director. I had to be undergraduate director. I founded the graduate program! I got it accredited! I pushed it through the Faculty Senate. I had to take care of students and younger faculty members. I hated all that administrative stuff! I'm still doing editing work for pay part-time now. And I have my writing. I love to write and need my writing time. No way am I doing all that free work at the blueberry farm!!! NO WAY!!!!!"

Evelyn looks shocked. She pats my shoulder. "We'll see what we can do, little human."

"Why don't you make the lattes!!!" I raise my voice again.

Bruce interjects. "Maybe we could just serve iced tea instead. Some with blueberry syrup, some plain." He's good at using the practical to smooth waters. Not sure it'll work this time, though. In any case, I know he agrees with me. He wants me to take it easier now that I'm no longer teaching. He's protective of my swim time and my writing time, as well as his own time off.

Evelyn starts explaining, "I can't work in the shop because I'll be helping Malcolm with gourmet food trips up to Lake Superior."

I'm yelling again. "I'm not working in a sweaty place while you swim up to Superior and eat gourmet food!!!"

Evelyn is patting faster, looking a bit lost. She stands up, faces the Lake, and lets out a loud "Eeeeeeeeeeeeeeeeeeeeeeeeeee."

I start hiccupping. Bruce takes over the shoulder patting. We all wait.

Malcolm appears. "What's wrong, honey bun?" he says to Evelyn.

"Maud is having a meltdown," she says.

Malcolm sits next to me. "Take a deep breath," he says. "Now another."

"I need a Kleenex," I say. Bruce hands me one from his pocket.

"Picture a happy place," Malcolm says.

"Yes, Oval Beach, Saugatuck, and I'm SWIMMING, not making lattes," I say, still irritated. No tears this time.

I take my prepared notes out of my purse. Prepared for the meeting, even before I knew Evelyn was going to be so bossy.

"OK, here's what I want. Listen. To. Me. We each take a week or two during blueberry season, July–August. I'm not taking more than two weeks. And I'm not organizing the Little Mermaids. And I'm not doing any of the ordering for the store like tea or coffee. I will deal with Michigan Conservation and get their educational materials. Also make some of our own bright and fun ones with stickers, as to our eco-efforts on the merman's farm. I need air conditioning in the store. I need an air-conditioned place to sleep. I stay up late and sleep late, so the store can only be open from about 2:00 to 6:00. And not every day. Maybe Monday and Tuesday it's closed for swimming. And I need a golf cart or a bus route to get to the beach."

I raise my voice again, "I REFUSE TO BE CHAIR! I'm not even getting a paycheck anymore." (I have some PTSD from my old academic job.)

Evelyn and Malcolm look a little shocked.

Bruce says, "These are very reasonable demands. I agree with Maud a hundred percent."

"We're going home now," I say. And Bruce and I do.

Episode 22
Road Trip!

Winter is the only time of the year when the 2 ½ hour drive from Chicago to Saugatuck is likely to take only 2 ½ hours. Bruce and I sleep in and then start our drive. The sky is gray, the highway shoulders patchy with ice, the trees bare, drivers edgy and cutting others off for no reason. Then as we begin to get disenchanted with the trip, we turn off I-94 onto I-196, lined with trees, beach grass, wild field edges, signs to vineyards, and turnoffs to beach towns, and we start feeling happy and excited. We remember, what the season denies in terms of swimming, it gives generously in terms of towns empty of tourists yet still stocked with hot coffee and muffins. Walking on wintry beaches. The light is eerie and starts bluing around 3:00 in the afternoon. The Lake is luminous.

This trip, Bruce and I decide to stay at the Best Western in Saugatuck, near Douglas. We arrive and, except for the Indian family who own and run it, it feels like we're almost the only ones there. Slightly south of us is Route 89. After unpacking we head on 89 due east to Crane's Pie Pantry Restaurant and Winery on the edge of Fennville for an early dinner. This is our trip to explore the merman's farm west of Fennville and scout out the rest of the area. Evelyn and Malcolm have agreed to take some weeks of blueberry season, July–August, and the merman has assured them we can run the air conditioning as much as we like, and also sleep at the farm as long as we stay downstairs and out of his upstairs spa. Everyone has gotten more relaxed and agreed to take it one step or tail thump at a time—and to share the work. Since they've been listening to me and showing themselves willing to divide the chores, I'm not angry anymore, just wary. We want to suss things out in advance of what could be a busy summer.

The next day around 2:00, Bruce and I are scheduled to meet S. at her farm Deelish Organics to get some tips. After a romantic night at the Best Western, and a quick brunch in Saugatuck at Uncommon Coffee, we drive over. Well, S. couldn't have been nicer. They don't do blueberries, so no competitiveness, and they'd been curious about their reclusive neighbor. We explain we haven't met him yet either and are just friends of friends of his, but are looking forward to helping out some at his mini-store this summer and learning more about eco-farming as well as distributing eco-literature. We show our true selves by admitting we're really looking forward to being as lazy as possible and getting some swimming in. S. laughs and shares that although she works hard, that's pretty much her long-term goal too. She shows us around, and we politely buy some of the root vegetables she has stored up.

Then we head back to Saugatuck and go for a walk on Oval Beach. No beach parking fee, no lifeguards, no other people! Hell of a sunset, though. We stop at Pennyroyal Cafe on our way back to the Best Western.

Finally, the following day is when we're slated to meet Evelyn and Malcolm on the porch of the merman farmer's house. At 2:00, natch—we don't do mornings. The farmer won't be there, but Evelyn and Malcolm have keys.

Turns out, I'm so glad to see those two mer-rascals! And they've brought presents, vintage seaweed helmets for Bruce and me. Those hats are toasty! Evelyn and Malcolm are in head-to-toe black down puffers, and we sensible Chicagoans have on our share of down too. Evelyn is quite excited. Malcolm is smiling pleasantly and keeps patting us on the shoulders. Evelyn opens the door, ta-da! We step in on the welcome mats. The place is spotless! It's decorated like a big city bachelor pad, all black, brown, and gray leather furniture, with stainless steel lamps and blonde, polished wooden floors. We take off our boots and slip on leather slippers provided for guests. Evelyn escorts us into the kitchen, again everything is new and gleaming. This time the floor is tiled in warm reds. She shows us the large refrigerator and freezer, to be shared over the summer, and the separate freezer for the farmer's raw fish only. On the counter are empty containers to be used for iced tea. In the cupboards are bottles of blueberry syrup from the farm's supply.

Proudly, Evelyn shows us the front room, fitted out with chairs, tables, a counter, and a cash-or-credit payment system, as well as a smaller fridge, and some shelves for educational materials and books.

There are not one but two guest bedrooms! New beds, beautiful linens.

I ask, "Where does he get the money to outfit his home like this?"

"Oh, this is nothing, you should see the spa upstairs! Except you won't because we had to promise to respect his privacy up there."

"Not a problem," says Bruce.

Malcolm answers my question. "The farm pays for itself. It turns a small profit, and most of the earnings go directly back into the farm and the house. It's a retreat for the mer-farmer as well as a farm, and I think that's wonderful. Also, as mentioned, he pays someone to come once a week to clean (and he pays them well), so you wouldn't have to worry about that during your weeks here, just try not to make a mess."

"I love this," I say. This place feels peaceful.

Malcolm says, "The farmer has been meaning to go more eco anyway, so is glad to have us bring in the Little Mermaids to plant the clover border, and for us to start the research process re: organic mulch covering for the early spring fertilizing. He's already thinking of switching to fish emulsion and feather meal for an organic fertilizer."

"He sees the educational materials (plus iced tea) as low key, something we could share with visitors and even other blueberry farmers if they're interested, but he doesn't want to do the outreach part to other farms, so that'd be up to us if the first summer or two work out. He said to tell you, though, to talk with Carlos who co-owns one of the other Fennville farms, Deelish Organics. As it happens, Carlos's parents were the first in the state of Michigan to have an organic blueberry farm!"

"Oh! We were just at Deelish Organics yesterday introducing ourselves to S.!" I say.

"Great, well, Carlos is her husband, you likely can meet him later in the summer," Malcolm adds.

"OK, human friends, put your shoes back on, we've got a surprise for you in the barn," Evelyn says, smiling kindly at us. This Evelyn on good behavior thing makes me a little nervous.

We trudge out, the frozen grass crackling under our boots. Evelyn hauls open the barn door. Just inside is a golf cart! "Look at what's hanging from the handle!" she says.

Bruce starts to move forward, but she waves him back. Takes me by the shoulder—gotta say, forcefully—and brings me to the left handle. Something laminated is hanging down. I turn it over. It says, Swimming Permit—Hutchins Lake.

"Woah! Wait a minute, wait a minute. I know about Hutchins Lake! It's not far from here, more in the woods closer to Fennville, and it's a good size."

"Exactly, little human! In the morning (if you're awake) or after work, you can buzz over there in the golf cart and swim to your heart's content!" She gives me a hug.

I have tears in my eyes. It's a Midwestern miracle!

Episode 23
Hutchins Lake

Fast forward to July.

Evelyn and I lie on our backs on the slatted swim float at the dock end of Hutchins Lake, which itself is not too far from the blueberry farm. I'm covering the store at the mer-farmer's house the last two weeks of the month, but today is a Monday, the store is closed, and Evelyn showed up promptly at 2:00 to golf cart with me over to Hutchins.

On the float, the water sluices off our bodies, the high-SPF sun block with it. This is the first time I'd seen the full length of Evelyn's legs up close. "Your legs are nice," I say, "but—hope you don't mind me saying—they look a little tall for your body."

"Yeah, well, your boobs look large for your body."

"That's just my body type. Besides I like my breasts."

"Well, I like my tail better than my legs. Have you seen my tail? Iridescent as fuck."

"Yeah, it's beautiful."

"Want to have sex?" Evelyn asks.

I wonder if she really wants to, or if it's her way of still trying to make up from our fight over workloads. "Oh, thanks," I say, "but I'm faithful to Bruce—we're monogamous."

Sigh. "Yeah, Malcolm and I are supposedly, too, but I figure we could chalk it up to inter-species diplomacy, and queer to boot."

"I'm just into Bruce." I add, "I think you're pretty, though, and sexy."

I ask, "Evelyn, have you ever made love to a woman, human or merwoman?"

"Oh, sure. Did you ever see that vampire TV series *True Blood* or read the Sookie-the-waitress books by Charlaine Harris it was based on?"

"Yes!" I reply. "I love the books especially. I'd love to meet Charlaine Harris sometime."

"Yeah, I was into the TV series and the books, too," Evelyn agrees. "OK, you remember how Charlaine Harris says that vampires are bisexual because they live so long, they've tried everything at least once? And for the hot ones, like Eric, many more times than once?"

"Yeah, delicious, it was like Eric was up for anything—that was part of his appeal."

"Well," continues Evelyn, "some of us mer-people are like that, too. I'm mainly hetero, but I keep an open mind."

"Cool," I say.

Evelyn says, "Hey, let's swim in, towel off, and get iced tea and blueberry muffins at the Hutchins Lake Inn."

Splash. Evelyn is in the water, not even bothering to change back to her tail for the short swim to the dock. She powers in with butterfly strokes. I take my time with a breaststroke, savoring the cool water after the hot sun, diving down to get my face cold and wash my hair back, and up to steadily push toward shore. We'd stuffed towels and cotton shifts, also linen summer sweaters and sandals, and discretely a couple of credit cards, not to mention my rescue inhaler, in the golf cart. After some toweling off and waving our arms and twirling around to semi-dry our suits, we put on the dresses and make our way to the Inn's café.

We both get blueberry-galore muffins with tons of blueberries and no added sugar, plus unsweetened tea, and sit on the porch indulging. "This is the life," says Evelyn.

"It really is," I respond.

Episode 24
The Shop Takes Shape

I have to work the blueberry farm eco-shop the next day, Tuesday. We've named it The Shop for Lazy Activists and Free Blueberry Iced Tea. Open Tues.–Sat., 2:00–6:00. We serve unsweetened iced tea and iced tea sweetened with blueberry syrup. We offer literature from FLOW, Michigan League of Conservation Voters, Oil & Water Don't Mix, the Environmental Protection Agency, and a bunch of other places, and our own one-page list—plus emoji stickers!—of what the farm is doing for sustainability and to prevent unhealthy runoff into the stream and the Lake. We've realized that people don't really like to be told what to do, so we also have a blueberry bush skeleton of wire with clothespins all over it and paper and pens nearby for people to leave suggestions about eco-farming or keeping the Lake clean. That's popular. More fun to offer suggestions than be lectured.

I'm all set for the next day with tea, seltzer, and blueberry syrup chilling in the big kitchen fridge, the sustainable cups out, the small freezer in the store stocked with ice.

The surprise the next morning—or morning to me, I don't get up till 10:30 or so, then shower and eat breakfast, so we're talking midday—is Evelyn is back with more baking supplies. She wants to try to make those no-sugar-added blueberry muffins we'd had at Hutchins Lake.

"Hey, you're not going away on Malcolm's July gourmet food trip?"

"Nope, someone has to keep an eye on you and this place."

I'm glad but play it cool, "Really? I thought it was going pretty smoothly."

"Yeah, well, also I'm disgusted Enbridge is going ahead with its plan to build a tunnel to transport oil and other chemicals right under the Straits. It's one step better than Line 5 just laying unprotected at the bottom of the water, but X told me that the model of tunnel plus pipe is unproven. And it still threatens the Lakes! I'm just taking a break from the whole thing and hanging out here in the southern part of the Lake, doing my thing. Malcolm can handle the tour and getting through the Straits just fine for now."

"Oh, yeah, I read about the tunnel. It's discouraging."

"That's why I love what we're doing, farm eco-improvement by farm eco-improvement, small notes on wire bushes by small notes on wire bushes, Little Mermaids planting clover, the farm switching to eco-fertilizer and eco-mulch. I figure next summer we could go around to other southwest Michigan farms, if you want to (she's being more polite now), and offer wire bushes for their stores and Little Mermaid volunteers for planting borders near streams. Maybe we'll get some 4-H clubs involved too."

"I'd love that. I'll work on that in my lazy activist way—as long as I have a lot of swimming breaks. Doesn't this all sound kind of cozy for you, though? I imagine you liking to smash things up."

"Well, I'm not against a spot of sabotage on the new tunnel, but you said you don't want to be involved in anything illegal."

"I appreciate your sensitivity, darlin'."

I'm going back and forth between the shop in the front and the kitchen in the back, finishing the store set up, when who do I see pull up in a car? Bruce! What the! I run out.

"OMG, I thought you had to work today."

"Surprise! I took some days off!"

Hugging, kissing, leaning against the car in true American deep summer, human style.

Evelyn yells from the kitchen, "Get a room!"

We have a few visitors over the course of the afternoon, and it's pleasant serving them iced tea and eco-literature, asking them to spread the word.

One of them, Cheyenne Sloan, MSU Extension Blueberry and Small Fruit Educator, stops in, as promised. Looking ahead, we've asked her to talk with us about organic pesticides. She warns, "There are organic pesticides available, but the main reason why organic management of blueberries can be tricky in Michigan is because of spotted wing drosophila (SWD) which is an invasive insect we have been dealing with in Michigan and across the country for several years now." But she adds encouragingly, "Not to say that organic production isn't possible—I know of a few organic producers in the area—there's just a lot more spraying than people might realize when working in an organic system."

We plan to meet up with her at the Kalamazoo agricultural extension office (where Cheyenne is housed) to learn more. She tells us to bring some blueberry iced tea when we do.

Later, Evelyn, Bruce, and I sit in wicker rockers on the merman's porch sampling iced tea and the mini-no-sugar-added-extra-blueberry blueberry muffins. (Yes, we stole the idea.)

Evelyn says, "Lemme ask you something, Maud: how come you take your rescue inhaler with you everywhere but you never use it?"

"Oh, I use my regular preventative inhaler every morning and every night to keep my asthma inflammation down, so I only need the rescue one if I get sick or if there's a lot of pollution. Like right now back in Chicago with the late-July sun and city heat, there's an increase in ozone, which, in addition to particulate pollution, can cause terrible asthma attacks. That's why I volunteered to work up here the second half of July. Though urban pollution is a problem at other times too. There's some here as well, but more in the city."

"Hmm," says Evelyn, "maybe we'll need to tackle particulate pollution in Chicago next."

"I'm in," says Bruce.

"Me, too," I agree. "No sabotage of Chicago factories or anything, though."

I see a glint in Evelyn's eye. "Well, you never know what the Little Mermaids will get up to."

Episode 25
Friends Measure Their Lungs

Evelyn never forgets anything. I wonder if she's a Scorpio, like me.

It's the beginning of October and unseasonably warm. Bruce and I show up at 57th Street beach around 2:30 with four beach towels, a thermos full of tea, and a box of Ube Crinkles from Tropicake. Evelyn and Malcolm are late.

"If they're much later, I'm eating their cookies," I say.

Bruce moves the box to his other side. "Look," he points.

On the horizon, there's a small wave approaching on the otherwise calm Lake. As it gets closer, we can see Evelyn and Malcolm doing butterfly strokes in parallel, causing wake, like from a motorboat. Closer still, their bronze faces gleam. They're laughing, racing toward the beach. I swear there's spray lifting off their wet hair. They stop for a minute when they hit the sandy shelf near the beach, hugging and wrestling over who won, catching their breath, and underwater changing into legs. They stride out and throw themselves on the towels we've laid out.

"Hi, little humans!" says Evelyn.

"Hey there!" from Malcolm.

"Wow, you two look like an advertisement for the freshwater mermaid way of life."

"Natch," says Evelyn, who is, after all, a Midwestern mermaid to boot and knows the lingo.

We chat and drink tea for a while. I don't get to eat their cookies.

"Hey, Maud, are you wearing a bathing suit and a sweater?"

I laugh, "Yeah, for wading out on the sandy shelf. The water's still a little warm, and the sun is bright, but the air is starting to cool off. So. . . ." I smile.

"Cool," says Evelyn.

"How's tap thumping going?" Malcolm asks Bruce.

"Pretty good, Calvin and I are performing later this month at City Lit Books. Like usual, I'm doing tap to his poetry. I've also got one piece where I do a poem of my own interspersed with tapping. You guys are welcome to come, if you want."

"For sure," Malcolm replies, "and could Evelyn read a poem?"

"Yeah, there's an open mic part. You have to come early and sign up, but then it all runs like clockwork."

"It's really fun," I add.

"Ah, I feel so lazy," Evelyn lies back on her towel. "Do we really have to have a meeting now?"

"Yep, I brought some equipment."

"Hmm," says Evelyn looking under her eyelashes at Malcolm, "sounds like some of my hookups on Chicago beaches." Malcolm serenely ignores her, although when I look down, I can see he's placed one hand around her ankle.

"No sex toys, unfortunately," I say, "just a stethoscope and a breathing tester, a kind of breathalyzer."

"Well, the stethoscope . . . I remember that played in one scenario," Evelyn says. Malcolm grabs the other ankle and flips her over. I wonder whether ankle play counts as exotic for merpeople.

Bruce puts his arm around my waist and draws me to him. I don't know if he's getting into the spirit or protecting me from their romping.

Things calm down.

"OK, first, I thought we'd listen to each other breathe," I say.

"Nah, I'm good," from Bruce, and "No, thanks," from Malcolm.

"Sure, I'm game," says Evelyn, "I'll listen to you first."

"OK, just put the stethoscope in your ears and then the device at the bottom—the resonator—on my back, different places where you think my lungs are." I stay seated and turn my back to her. "Tell me when you're ready and I'll take some deep breaths so you can hear. This is one of the things they do at the asthma doctor's to see if you're breathing OK."

Evelyn puts the disc-shaped resonator down by my waist.

"No, move it to the upper half of my back. And listen for any wheezing please." She does, while I breathe deeply, in through my nose, blowing out hard through my mouth. She moves the resonator around.

"Sounds good to me," she says.

"OK, my turn."

She sits on my towel with her back to me. "You can start below my waist," she instructs.

I do. "OMG, your lungs are huge!" I move the stethoscope around while she imitates my deep breathing and then some. It sounds like someone is hitting a bass drum. It seems like her lungs fill her entire back.

"Amazing, Bruce, you have to hear this."

Bruce listens. "Wow."

We're humbled.

Evelyn explains, "Our lungs are large and powerful because we breathe above the water's surface, then dive down, and need to be able to stay under for long periods of time."

"That's so cool," I say.

Next, we try the breathalyzer. "You breathe in and then blow out through the instrument as hard and long as you can. You do that a few times and then average it. Sometimes we people with asthma can't get enough oxygen because of inflammation—this is especially true if there are allergy triggers in the air like pollen or air pollution or when we have a virus or right after recovery." I demonstrate, the others look on politely.

Next, Bruce takes a turn. His breathing capacity is better than mine, but mine is OK as my asthma is under control at the moment. I wipe off the breathalyzer and offer it to Malcolm. He modestly waves it away. "Let Evelyn try this one, too," he says.

I repeat the instructions. Evelyn takes in a deep breath, puts her mouth to the breathalyzer, and blows.

And the breathalyzer comes apart in many plastic pieces.

"OMG," Bruce says.

"Fuck," I say.

Malcolm laughs.

"I could've blown even harder," Evelyn brags.

There are some moments of silence.

"Alrighty then," I say. "You two have enormously powerful lungs! Good!!" I pause. "I think this also means, though, that since the interior surface area of your lungs is large, it can absorb a great deal of particulate matter into your bodies, which is not a good thing. PM is also not a good thing for those of us with smaller lungs than yours—for sure not for me as it can set off my asthma, and not for Bruce either as it can cause inflammation in his lungs, too, although to a lesser extent than mine."

Evelyn lies back down on her towel and watches the clouds. "Well, then," she says after a while, "particulate pollution is the enemy. I'm willing to take it on, but there have to be blueberry muffins and other treats involved."

I couldn't agree more.

Episode 26
Evelyn and Maud Email

From: justmaud@poetmail.com

To: coolerthanhumans@mermail.com

Evelyn, I've been researching online and it seems like to really get rid of particulate matter (PM), we'd need to eliminate gas-powered cars or greatly reduce their use in Chicago and amp up bike lanes, bike safety, and use of e-powered micro-mobility vehicles (like our beloved golf cart but electric). Also hugely increase the use of mass transit.

This seems like a tall order for us lazy activists!

We do well with activities where there's snacks, coffee or tea, and swimming, let's face it. Also joking around. And poetry.

Plus, this summer, we'll be back at the blueberry farm, running the store and the organic-suggestion tree, and spreading the word to other nearby farm shops, seeing if they want suggestion trees too. We'll be busy, so we'd better not bite off more than we can chew.

Whew. What to do. Well, with the bike thing we could try to improve one neighborhood and connect with others also working on things like getting concrete protectors for bike lanes installed in other neighborhoods. My nephew Carter is doing admirable things like this in Oakland, CA, and I'm sure he could give us some pointers.

BUT, I don't bike and I'm guessing neither do you since you prefer swimming to doing a lot of exercise with your temporary legs. Maybe our PM fight won't have to do with biking.

I get pleasure out of working to improve things related to

what I enjoy (not biking). I'll share this: my favorite philosopher is Ernst Bloch. He wrote about being inspired by *Spuren*, German for "traces," traces from the past that exist or can be remembered in the present and help us imagine a better future. And more: about how the past, present, and future can be all experienced in a montaged way at the same time. Swimming is like that for me. I love being in the water and moving through it, remembering at times doing so in my childhood, wanting in the future for there to be clean lakes to swim in, and for others to swim in.

So, what are our traces here?

Yours in swimming, Maud

From: coolerthanhumans@mermail.com
To: justmaud@poetmail.com
Maud, I like this traces thing. Well, for land memories, I like fucking guys on the beach, and some of those memories come back at times. Not sure how this can help us get rid of particulate matter in the air.

I'm at the spa below the Crib near 57th Street beach. About to get glitter strands put in my hair. Gotta go.

Or else, Evelyn

From: justmaud@poetmail.com
To: coolerthanhumans@mermail.com
Evelyn, ooh, glitter strands. I'd love some of those. Bet you'll look great in them.

No worries re the traces and the eco-work. I've got some traces/memories in mind that relate to the subway! I was thinking how in other cities where I've lived I took the subway often, but here in Chicago I avoid it. In NYC it was the fastest way to get around and everyone of all races and ages and social classes took the subway. I liked the mix. The cars and platforms were almost never deserted so I felt safe. It wasn't exactly clean, but it still felt friendly and well attended. In

Chicago, except at rush hour, platforms can be deserted, same with the cars themselves, and that doesn't feel safe to me. I like lots of people around.

Then I was thinking about the amazing, amazing subway systems in Singapore (where I lived for a semester), in Hong Kong (where I've visited a handful of times), and in Berlin (where I lived off and on for two years). In these cities the subways are CLEAN, they are used by a whole variety of people, they are safe, they are fast, they are even fun to use.

What if we got permission from the mayor's office or the CTA or whatever and took over ONE car and made it fun to be in???

Warmly,

Maud

To: justmaud@poetmail.com

From: coolerthanhumans@mermail.com

Maud, just wait till you see the glitter strands. They're fab. And I got a couple of extra in blue and silver for you and instructions on how to braid them into short hair. I'll dress your hair for you!

I don't want to throw water, haha, on your subway fantasy, but there's no way I'm going below water level on land. When I dive deep it's gotta be in the Lake. It's so beautiful there! The different shades of blue and green, the sunshine filtering down and the dark looming up, the fish swimming by, even the little invasive mussels busy taking over the bottom of the Lake where they don't belong but they're cute anyway. The pockets of cold and warmth in the water. Swimming through them.

Let's think of something more joyous and full of traces for our PM project.

Or else,

Evelyn

<h1 style="text-align:center">Episode 27
Back to the necessary</h1>

Evelyn comes bouncing in. "Hiya, Maud!" She pulls off her wool hat, her hair, now below her chin, comes down, and the glitter strands look amazing. I tell her so.

"Wait till you see them on you, lil human!"

She gets her order—a large latte, regular milk, if you must know—and sits down. I sip my flat white.

After a gulp or two, she pulls out my present. "Oh, those are beautiful," I exclaim.

"Now, I asked the stylist and she said for short hair, put these in the back, near the crown of the head, three or four strands, then they can spill out, or be tied in a ponytail."

"I love them."

Evelyn sets to work. There's a scent of pine resin, which I guess is the fixative.

Kate, necessary's owner, comes over to watch. "I love those," she says.

"Mmm," says Evelyn. Her mouth is full of bobby pins.

"Now, that's not a chemical smell, is it?" Kate asks, protective of her café.

"Nope," says Evelyn, "all organic pine."

"Oh, cool," says Kate, "sounds safe."

"It is," replies Evelyn.

Kate, supportive of women entrepreneurs, says, "OK, if it works well and you ever package it to sell, let's talk."

"Sure, thanks."

"I'll leave you to it," says Kate. I give her a thumbs up, she gives one back.

Evelyn stays busy with the strands.

"There!" announces Evelyn. I run into the bathroom to look and come out beaming.

"These are so pretty, thanks, Evelyn!"

"You look dazzling, lil human!"

"I'm going to show Erma and get us some ube bread."

Erma is at her Tropicake shop set up near the entrance. She oohs and ahs over the glitter strands, claims she wants some, too.

"Come meet my friend Evelyn," I say.

"Just for a minute, while there aren't more customers," Erma replies.

Erma and Evelyn get to talking and Erma starts telling her all the baking she has planned for Thanksgiving. "Yum," says Evelyn. Then Erma has to hurry back to her shop corner.

"I've got it," declares Evelyn, "we don't tell people to ride mass transit, we thank them for riding it."

"I love this direction—it's like our suggestion tree for organic berry farming. People don't like to be told what to do, they like to participate. In this case, be thanked. Tell me more."

"That's what I've got for now . . ."

We sit quietly for a while, sipping our drinks, eating our ube bread, and from time to time shaking our heads so the glitter strands fly around and sparkle.

This, natch, is the perfect brainstorming environment.

"I know!" I say. "We go to bus stops, the South Loop in particular, so it's neighborhood specific and cozy. And we thank people at the bus stops for taking mass transit, and hand out one 20 percent discount card for each person on one small baked item from Tropicake when bought from Erma's shop at necessary and sufficient coffee! That way, Kate and Erma get extra traffic into necessary. And we donate a certain amount to Erma to cover the discount cost. $200? Or something like that—we'd have to figure it out with her."

"Love it!" says Evelyn. "I could hand those out. Where do we get the $200?"

"Hmm, we'll think about it."

We shake our heads in the light some more. Life is good.

Episode 28
Evelyn and Maud at the Drawing Board

It's getting to be toward Halloween, but I still like to sneak in some wading time at 57th St. beach. In my usual off-season Lake Michigan getup of a sweater (or two) over my bathing suit. Gray day, upper 40s, there are so few people at the beach, Evelyn doesn't even bother to change out of her tail. She says if anyone comes by and asks, she'll tell them it's a new kind of wetsuit. Face it, days like this, we own this beach. Us and the Chicago Park District.

Bruce and Malcolm have once again gone to break into the Fieldhouse on Promontory Point to practice tap dancing. Malcolm is interested in performing with Bruce sometime, says it'd be a growth experience.

Gotta admit, the water feels plenty cold. I'm dreaming of our thermoses and towels on the beach. Still, I love being in the water. And Evelyn is totally comfortable, wearing her vintage seaweed hat and backstroking around while we talk.

"OK," I start, "to earn the $200, let's sell some stuff at necessary coffee. How about the pine fixative for the hair strands plus, natch, some strands?"

Evelyn gets practical. "The pine fixative takes forever to make and the strands I'd have to buy from my hairdresser, so I'm not sure that's the best way to go. But I like the idea of selling some handmade stuff at necessary. Kate seems nice."

"Yeah, she is. Well, what about that face cream or exfoliant you were mentioning a while ago, made up of those little mussels that've taken over the bottom of the Lake?"

"Oh, I love that stuff. It might, though, be too rough for human skin. See how you're shivering while I'm floating and relaxed? Human skin is thin."

"Yeah, it's time for me to get out and drink some hot tea."

Evelyn good-naturedly changes into her legs and gets out with me. We wrap in towels (in my case, a pile of them) and sip tea, looking out over the Lake.

"What I'd really like to make and sell," I say dreamily, "is lead-free, organic cocoa powder."

"Yeah, what's with the lead in cocoa powder?"

"Something about the way the big companies process it. There are some smaller ones like Navitas Organics, where I get mine, that make safer cocoa powder, with only small amounts of lead. I wonder if handmade could be lead free?"

"You love cocoa powder, right?"

"So much. I'd buy something like that. Bet other people would too."

"All right, let's research it. Meanwhile, what about a poetry and tap reading somewhere?? Gray days, let's get loud!"

"Yeah, why don't we."

Episode 29
Back at Westley's

It's the end of the month, right before Halloween, so it's time to catch Westley's open-mic evening for readings at Gallery Cabaret. Evelyn and I feel we deserve a break after brainstorming the thank-you for riding mass transit project. We love breaks. We round up Bruce, Malcolm, and Calvin to participate. Calvin's partner Jin is still commuting to her photography professor job at Illinois State and too busy to create something new for the evening, but she says she'll come relax with a beer. Bruce will be tap dancing along with poetry reads by first Calvin and then Malcolm at Westley's evening. Evelyn and I have committed to read one poem each.

We get there and no one at Gallery Cabaret is in a Halloween costume! Evelyn and I, though, are dressed as each other. I'm wearing my new shiny, blue-black mermaid tights, a black velvet top, and a wig with long black hair and some tinsel strands. Evelyn is wearing flowered velvet pants, a black velvet top, a wig with short hair and some hairdresser glitter strands, also make up to turn her cheeks pink and her eyes almond-shaped and smoky. The guys have refused to dress up although Calvin is looking natty in his sweater vest, and Bruce and Malcolm wear different colored Henleys, Bruce's blue and Malcolm's maroon. Westley, as always, is gracious, and chill.

Some other writers go first, and Westley himself reads some prose. Then he calls on us. Evelyn bounds up.

"Hi, you all, I grew up in Ohio, outside of Canton, and was in 4-H," she says. (OMG, I realize she's going to pretend to be me, not just dress like me.) "I was a writer and editor in New York City," she continues, "and then a professor at an art school in Chicago, and now I'm doing writing and editing again, also going to the beach a lot. And I love chocolate, especially cocoa powder."

Evelyn proceeds to read a poem I'd shared with her:

When the What Ifs Turn into Nows [Roi Fainéant, June 23, 2024]

What if I stayed up as late as I wanted to every night
and slept in as late as I wanted to each morning.
What if I wrote an eco-novel with more mermaids
and jokes than pollution data and activism.
What if I dressed up in reds head to toe, the next day
maroons, and my flowered velvet pants, to go to the café.
What if I invited all the Midwest writers I like from northern
    Wisconsin
to southern Ohio to read at my Chicago READINGS series.
And then with some of them, well, we become pals.
With others, I just wave them on their way, Midwestern nice.
I hear all of them, and sometimes read my own work, too.
What if, I refuse to use the phone, texts and emails only.
What if, I only hang out in places where races mix,
Jazz Showcase, Printers Row Wine Bar, 57th Street beach,
because it feels better, and my whole body relaxes.
What if I swim in Lake Michigan, worship the Lake, make love
to the Lake, stroke the Lake, splash the Lake, duck my head under.
What if I'm unafraid to tell people how much I love their writing,
when I love their writing, and I enjoy reading them.
What if I tell Bruce how much I love him and what a slut he is,
every day, he is that beautiful, inside and out.
What if I also keep in touch with my old friends,
my hometown neighbor since I was five and she was six,
my grade-school boyfriend, the twins I hung out with in high school.
What if I decide to forgive my hometown and embrace it,
even while it shrinks back into the cornfields.
What if I keep and make friends of different ages,

because life is more interesting that way.
What if I love to write, so I do, and edit a little on the side.
What if I go to readings around town, listening and reading
my own work, shy, but feel glorious while performing.
What if I mask at gallery openings, daring to be uncool.
What if I wear my hair, undercut, and weird.
What if I eat my sliced fruit with cocoa powder on it,
and get it everywhere. And am cocoa scented.
What if I have way less money, but zero faculty meetings to attend.
What if I sleep better at night, and more,
and read more mysteries. What if I go for a walk each day,
using my walking sticks. What if I'm old and I use that
to know life is short and devote mine to love,
cocoa powder, friendship, laziness, writing, readings. A touch of
  revenge.
What if you come visit, read at my READINGS series at the wine
  bar,
dress up any way you feel like, and come have a latte with me at the
  café?

Evelyn takes a deep bow.

Hmm, I go up on stage next and try to wing some opening patter in Evelyn's style.

"Hi, everybody. I'm wet and wild but secretly a sweetheart with really sharp teeth. I summer in Fennville, Michigan on a blueberry farm that's slowly going organic. I love to swim, and I spend a lot of time in the Lake. I do an awesome butterfly stroke—I challenge anyone here to a race."

I wink at the audience.

I read a new poem by Evelyn, fortunately I have it on my phone. The audience loves it.

I'm a Poet by Evelyn

I'm a poet, so do what I say
Go to the beach

Lay on a beach towel
Take all your clothes off
Even your wedding ring
Especially your wedding ring.
Oh, wait, I've moved on.
I'm a poet and I'm with Malcolm.
Malcolm, do what I say.
No? OK, then please make me a gourmet dinner.
Me? No, I don't cook. I eat!
I'm a poet and I eat.
First, I eat Malcolm. (You know what I mean.)
Then, I want wild rice from the
Bad River Band of Lake Superior Chippewa rez.
Boiled.
I'm a poet, and over that rice I want
RAW fish, whitefish and salmon,
No skin, but I'll take the heads in the mix
For extra crunch.
Mmm, EAT IT RAW, EAT IT RAW!!!

(I point the mic at the audience and they join in.)

"EAT IT RAW! EAT IT RAW!"

(And again.)

"EAT IT RAW! EAT IT RAW!"

I sit down. Evelyn and I giggle. Evelyn shows her incisors. Every game has an edge with Evelyn.

Then it's the tap-and-poetry guys' turn. What can I say? The Bruce tapping and Calvin reading combo is beautiful. Bruce stays on stage, Malcolm comes up, and to my surprise they tap together, then take a short break, Bruce reads some prose paying tribute to Gregory Hines, historic and iconic Chicago-born tap dancer, and then he and Malcolm resume their tap duet.

Huge applause from the whole bar, and a certain amount of standing up cheering and booming from Evelyn and me. "Goooooooooo guys!" we yell. I break out a few moves I remember from Ohio high school cheerleading, even though I wasn't a cheerleader. Arms up in a V, left arm out, right folded to the chest, right arm out, left folded to the chest. Arms back to the V! Evelyn jumps up and down which is a little scary since her jumps are high ones.

Fortunately, the rest of the audience is several drinks into the evening and doesn't seem to notice how high she goes. Everyone stands up and cheers.

Westley says, "Groovy, man."

Episode 30
Early Nov. on Promontory Park and Everything Wraps Up with a Bow—For Now

Evelyn and I are sitting on some rocks bordering Promontory Point. Before this, we were walking around the Point leaf peeping at the early November red-and-orange displays the trees offered. From every angle beneath the trees' branches, the Lake was visible. Then Evelyn got tired of using her legs and brought us to the rocks. She bounded down to some comfy ones to sit on. I followed gingerly.

"Evelyn," I say, "I have some bad news about our plan to earn $200 to pay Erma for discounting baked goods and us giving out coupons for that at bus stops."

"OK, I'm ready," she replies.

"I don't think, in our lazy way, we can make cocoa powder to sell." I take a deep breath. "I've been reading this great book called *Cocoa*, by Kristy Leissle, and, long story short, we'd have to buy the beans, ferment them, heat them up, remove the husks and stuff, separate the cocoa butter from the other stuff, and then grind the other stuff to make cocoa powder. And we'd need machinery for a lot of that."

"Hmm, that's not happening," says Evelyn.

"Then," I continue, "I was Googling around the internet and I came on blueberry extract which is much, much easier to make, basically blueberries and vodka left to soak for 4–5 weeks, strained, and there you have it." Evelyn perks up. "But you need a license to sell alcohol, so I think rather than get that, which is costly, and try to sell the extract, maybe it'd be better just to make some as a present for the merman for being so hospitable to us and the shop in the summer."

Evelyn leaps into the water, wiggles around, and I can see dimly beneath the water's surface her tail forming. "Ah, that's better," she says. "Well, maybe we won't go around thanking people for riding mass transit. I mean, do we have to do *everything*?"

"Yeah, I agree, I think we can just use the winter to prep more wire trees for farm stores near Fennville to receive organic farming tips—and emoji-covered sheets saying what the merman farm is already doing and wants to do. And maybe get our no-sugar-added blueberry muffin recipe down. That kind of thing. Do more poetry and tap performances, write some stories, relax, have fun. Invent a little magic."

"Oh, I know some magic I could teach you."

"You mean, like, real magic?" I ask, "not human magic tricks?"

"Yeah, real magic."

"So cool! I'm all ears."

"Lemme ask my mermaid group what I can show you and what's off-limits for humans."

"Deal."

"Deal."

"OK, let's gossip now, then. Ask me anything."

"How old are you?"

"Not telling," Evelyn says. "Older than you. Ask me gossip about other people."

Sigh. "Alrighty, why, really does the merman live in Fennville? Besides getting away from his family?"

"He's gay and likes to go cruising in Saugatuck. Also, he loves to farm."

"He's gay? I thought you went out with him."

"Sure, yeah, I told you, some of us mer-people are very open."

"Now you ask me something," I say.

"Are we going to stick to lazy activism directly about the Lake and its water?"

"Yep," I say. "After all, we're both a water sign. We're Scorpios."

"Agreed. Hey, how did you know that?"

"I have my own magic, a kind of sixth sense," I say, trying to sound mysterious. (Evelyn looks impressed.) "My turn," I continue. "Are you going to tell X Moder you're a mermaid?"

"Probably. Want to go visit her?"

"For sure. Her dad Tim invited me to do a reading up in a coffee shop in Duluth so maybe we can coordinate then, I think the Bad River Band reservation is only a couple of hours away. You and Malcolm could swim up, Bruce, Tim, and I could drive from Duluth."

"Yeah, sounds good, maybe in the spring. OK, my turn," says Evelyn. "Do you think we'll ever write some poetry together?"

"I'd love to!"

"Same! I have another question, Maud."

"No way, it's my turn," I assert.

"Are you and Malcolm going to make a baby?" I ask.

"Do I seem like the kind of person who wants to take care of a baby? Are you and Bruce?"

"No way. Plus, I'm too old. Also, you answered a question with a question."

"You could adopt."

"Nope. Not against adoption, just against changing diapers."

"My turn again," says Evelyn.

"No." Evelyn splashes me. "It's still my turn," I say undaunted. "You're OK with my publishing our adventures?" I ask.

"Yeah, I trust you. Just show me the manuscript beforehand so I can take out any details that are too revealing. Also, please call it a fantasy book so readers will think it's made up even though it's not."

"Deal."

"Now, finally my turn again," says Evelyn. "Do you think I'll become a painter?"

"Nope, too many supplies to keep dry. Writing poetry is easier for someone jumping between water and land and living in the water."

"That makes sense. Poetry is my open road," Evelyn says while looking dramatically out at the horizon.

"Hey," she adds, "there's the Crib where we first met."

"A beautiful sight," I reply.

"To more adventures in the future," Evelyn says. "To swimming. And saving the Lake! And goofing off a lot. And friendship."

"For sure," I say, in Midwesternese.

Evelyn swims off with a wink and a wave.

Appendix, Resources

Clean Water Organizations, Websites

This resource list contains some national and regional organizations, but leans toward local ones based in Illinois and Michigan, places where our Lazy Activists spend most of their time when on land. For information on organizations based in the other Great Lakes states, please see River Network's Great Lakes Drinking Water Advocates Database, rivernetwork.org.

Alliance for the Great Lakes, greatlakes.org
Bay Mills Indian Community, baymills.org/enbridge-
     information-portal
Bad River Band of Lake Superior Chippewa, Ashland, WI,
     badriver-nsn.gov
Blacks in Green, blacksingreen.org
Delta Institute, delta-institute.org
Detroit Jews for Justice, detroitjewsforjustice.org
Earth Justice (Midwest), earthjustice.org/office/Midwest
East Michigan Environmental Council (EMEAC), emeac.org
Ecology Center, Ann Arbor, MI, ecocenter.org
Elevate, elevatenp.org
Environmental Law & Policy Center, elpc.org/states/Illinois
Environmental Protection Agency, Region 5, Chicago, epa.
     gov/aboutepa/epa-region-5
Faith in Place, faithinplace.org
farmland.org
Flint Development Center, flintdc.org
Flint Rising Coalition (project of The Advocacy Fund),
     flintrising.com

Freshwater Lab, UIC, freshwaterlab.org, director Rachel
    Havrelock
FLOW: For Love of Water, Traverse City, MI, forloveofwater.org
Freshwater Future, freshwaterfuture.org
Great Lakes Commission, glc.org
Great Lakes Environmental Law Center, glelc.org
Great Lakes Info Network (GLIN), glc.org
Great Lakes Now, greatlakesnow.org
Great Lakes PFAS Action Network (GLPAN), glpan.org
Healing Our Waters (HOW) Great Lakes Coalition,
    healthylakes.org
Huron River Watershed Council, hrwc.org
Hydrate Detroit, hydratedetroit.org
Illinois Environmental Council, ilenviro.org
Illinois-Indiana Sea Grant, ilseagrant.org
Little Village Environmental Justice Organization, lvejo.org
Michigan Citizens for Water Conservation, savemiwater.org
Michigan Environmental Council, environmentalcouncil.org
Michigan League of Conservation Voters, Ann Arbor, MI,
    michiganlcv.org
National Wildlife Federation's Great Lakes Regional Center,
    nwf.org
Native American Rights Fund, narf.org
Natural Resources Defense Council, nrdc.org
Nature Conservancy, Michigan, Water, nature.org/en-us/
    about-us/where-we-work/united-states/michigan/stories-
    in-michigan/protect-water/
NWF—Great Lakes Center, nwf.org
Oil & Water Don't Mix, oilandwaterdontmix.org
People's Water Board Coalition, peopleswaterboard.org
Pilsen Environmental Rights and Reform Organization
    (PERRO), pilsenperro.org
Prairie Rivers Network, prarierivers.org
River Network, rivernetwork.org
River Raisin Watershed Council, riverraisin.org

Sierra Club—IL Chapter, sierraclub.org
Sloan, Cheyenne, MSU Extension Blueberry & Small Fruit Educator, Kalamazoo Extension Office
Southeast Environmental Task Force, setaskforce.org
Tip of the Mitt Watershed Council, watershedcouncil.org
Trevor Nichols Research Center, Fennville, MI, canr.msu.edu

Books

Benton-Banai, Edward, *The Mishomis Book: The Voice of the Ojibway* (U of Minnesota Press, 2010)
Coleman, Elliot, *The New Organic Grower: A Master's Manual of Tools and Techniques for the Home and Market Gardener*, 30th Anniversary Edition (Chelsea Green Publishing, 2018)
Cothron, Blake, *The Berry Grower: Small Scale Organic Fruit Production in the 21st Century* (New Society Publishers, 2022)
Egan, Dan, *The Death and Life of the Great Lakes* (W.W. Norton & Co., 2017)
Elder, Jane E., *Wilderness, Water & Rust: A Journey Toward Great Lakes Resilience* (Michigan State University Press, 2024)
Leissle, Kristy, *Cocoa* (Polity, 2018)
Treuer, Anton, *Ojibwe in Minnesota* (Minnesota Historical Society Press, 2010)
Warren, William W., *History of the Ojibway People*, edited and annotated with an introduction by Theresa Schenck (Minnesota Historical Society Press, 1885/2009)

Acknowledgements

I'd like to thank Evelyn for her friendship and for keeping me good company throughout these adventures and this writing. And much gratitude to Bruce Black, Zach Cahill, and Tim Moder for reading part or all of this manuscript and offering comments and suggestions. Poet Tim Moder also reviewed the Chippewa material and the poetry in this book, and I'm so grateful to him. My thanks to climate change scientist Dr. Mika Tosca for reviewing the eco-information in the book. I'd like to thank Ryan Griffis for additions to the appendix. I'm very grateful to Mike Phillips, EIC, and From Beyond Press for publishing this novel. And I thank artist Iris Bernblum for her Evelyn-esque (there is no higher compliment) cover art.

Parts of this novel were given as readings in Chicago at Printers Row Wine in the South Loop, Semicolon Books in the Loop, and City Lit Books in Logan Square, and I thank Tanya Gentile, Ada Cheung, and Carrie McGath respectively for their hospitality at each.

My thanks to *Portable Gray*, the journal of University of Chicago's Gray Center for the Arts and Inquiry, for publishing a short excerpt from the novel in Spring 2024, to *Copihue Poetry* for publishing the "Ladybug" poem in 2023, and to *Roi Fainéant* for publishing the poem "When the What Ifs Turn into Nows" in June 2024.

My love to Lake Michigan and especially 57th Street beach on Chicago's South Side—and always to my partner in love, eroticism, adventure, and beach time Bruce Black.

About the Author

A Pushcart Prize and Best of the Net nominee, Maud Lavin has published in *BULL*, *Cowboy Jamboree*, *Reckon Review*, *Copihue Poetry*, *BRIDGE*, *Harpy Hybrid*, *Roi Fainéant*, the *Nation*, *Harper's Bazaar*, *Slate*, and other venues. One of her books, *Cut with the Kitchen Knife* (Yale UP), was named a New York Times Notable Book. Her other books include *Clean New World* and *Push Comes to Shove* (both MIT Press), *Silences, Ohio* (Cowboy Jamboree Press), and three anthologies. Her writing has appeared in Chinese, Japanese, Korean, German, Dutch, Finnish, and Spanish as well as English. She is a 4-H alumna and a Guggenheim Fellow.